ONE DOWN

This was one killing Douchane was figuring on enjoying. He had gunned down a lot of men in duels, but he never had wanted to kill anyone as much as this green kid who dared challenge him.

The trouble was, the kid's gun blazed first. Douchane staggered. He was hit. The damn fellow was amazingly fast. But there was no pain. So not a bad wound.

Douchane tried to complete the raising of his pistol. It was terribly heavy. He began to lean to the side. His face plowed into the grass of the meadow.

The onlookers stood open-mouthed. The kid, Tom Gallatin, was the fastest draw they ever saw. The duel was more an execution than a contest.

Tom was settling the score—one bullet at a time. . . .

The Shanghaiers

by
F. M. Parker

A SIGNET BOOK

NEW AMERICAN LIBRARY

Copyright © 1987 by F. M. Parker

All rights reserved. For information address Doubleday & Company, Inc., 245 Park Avenue, New York, New York 10167.

This is an authorized reprint of a hardcover edition published by Doubleday & Company, Inc.

SIGNET TRADEMARK REG. U.S. PAT. OFF. AND FOREIGN COUNTRIES
REGISTERED TRADEMARK—MARCA REGISTRADA
HECHO EN CHICAGO, U.S.A.

SIGNET, SIGNET CLASSIC, MENTOR, ONYX, PLUME, MERIDIAN and NAL BOOKS are published by NAL PENGUIN INC., 1633 Broadway, New York, New York 10019

First Signet Printing, February, 1988

1 2 3 4 5 6 7 8 9

PRINTED IN THE UNITED STATES OF AMERICA

PROLOGUE—THE MAKING OF THE LAND

One colossal continent, Pangaea, held all the land of the great planet that was Earth. A mighty, restless sea miles deep covered the remainder of the world.

Pangaea, composed of granite-like slag, had existed for many millions of years. This huge crustal plate was sixty miles thick and rested upon the basalt of the deeper mantle of the globe.

The earth was already immensely old, more than four billion years, when the one huge continent existed. It was not the first supercontinent to have coalesced upon the surface of the earth, only the last.

Two hundred million years ago the hot flows of softened rock in the Earth's mantle, fueled and stirred by the planet's own internal heat, began to swirl upward with irresistible currents. Pangaea fractured and shattered into seven huge blocks and several smaller ones.

Antarctica, Australia and the Indian subcontinent broke loose first. Then Africa and the Americas pulled free. The fragments of Pangaea drifted apart, an inch or two each year, upon the dense basalt of the hot seafloor.

One of the new landforms, the North American Plate that included half of the Atlantic Ocean, moved westward. It collided with a section of the Pacific floor, a mass of the planet's crust that extended to Japan and was rafting north.

At the crushing, slamming contact of the two gigantic plates, a fault zone seventy-five miles deep and nineteen hundred miles long was created between them.

The forces of the plates pressing upon each other were beyond imagination. The compression crumpled the leading edge of the North American Plate and thrust up tall mountains with scores of craggy peaks.

The friction on the opposing walls of the fault was so great it locked the crustal blocks together for long periods. Then at times somewhere deep within the bowels of the earth the stress would exceed the strength of the rocks, the final linchpin would break, and the two disputing sides of the crustal plates would bound forward with awesome might. Massive quantities of rock were jerked and torn, the rents rising to the very surface of the planet and splitting mountain ranges as if they were the feeblest of sand hills.

During these earthquakes, the land surface rolled like waves of the sea, and shook and joggled. Sometimes the contending sides of the fault would gape open and then snap close like the jaws of some giant, angry beast. Sulfurous fumes from molten cauldrons within the mantle escaped up along the momentarily open fissure. Some of the earthquake wave energy would burst free of the rock of the earth crust and agitate and whip the molecules of air into incredible explosions of noise.

The total planet trembled at the battle of the giants for first right of passage across the face of the Earth. It trembled countless times over the millions of years the crustal plates waged their never-ending war. During these aeons, the western side of the fault, grinding north at two inches per year, has traveled three hundred and fifty miles past the eastern wall.

The mountains of the North American Plate cut crosswise the path of the prevailing storms that drove in from the west, forcing the moisture-laden air to rise abruptly. And the sky-brushing crown of the Sierra Nevada Mountains milked the clouds, wringing billions upon billions of gallons of water from them to fall upon the land.

The water rushed down from the rocky crags of the mountains and collected into rivulets, which grew into creeks that merged to form mighty rivers. For countless thousands of years, the ancient ancestor rivers of the Sacramento and the San Joaquin cut and carved wide valleys to carry their prodigious currents. And the millennia passed, score after score, adding to millions of years.

Early in their lives, the two rivers had joined their flows in a large valley near the coast. Then the doubly strong currents of the streams fought the great fault that many times shifted and jostled their beds and tried to dam their passage. Always they pounded a channel through the upthrown ridges and kept open a deep, broad gorge to the sea.

As the Pacific Plate continued to drive north, the land near the ocean lowered. The salty brine of the sea flooded to fill the valleys of the Sacramento and San Joaquin rivers for many miles up their course. Several hills near the river were inundated until only their topmost crest poked above the water to form islands in the newly created bay.

That is the way man found the land.

He named the sunken, flooded river channels the San Francisco Bay. The deeply carved gorge leading to the sea between the peninsula headlands became the Golden Gate.

San Francisco was the name man gave the city he built by the bay.

Chapter 1

The judge of duels looked at his watch in the dim light of dawn slowly coming to Angel Island. He repocketed the timepiece. It was not yet the appointed moment. The killing would have to wait a little longer. He wrapped his thick wool cape tightly about himself to ward off the cold, damp wind coming off San Francisco Bay.

The surgeon stood silently beside the judge, near the center of a small meadow sloping down to the bay. He stared south across the water toward the city of San Francisco. His leather satchel containing medicines and sharp steel scalpels and probes was at his feet.

One of the duelists, Captain Douchane, the master of the clipper ship *Sierra Wind*, was near the water's edge. He was watching his vessel at anchor some four miles away and just off the end of The Embarcadero. Miniaturized by the distance, the clipper was a toy ship with three bare masts.

Cochran, the *Sierra Wind*'s first officer and

Douchane's second for the duel, was beside his captain. He held a flat wooden box in his hand.

The second duelist, Tom Gallatin, stood up the slope of the meadow at the base of the lone hill that made Angel Island. He was a tall, wiry young man with black hair. Tan Ke was with him. The Chinaman had a holstered pistol with the gun belt coiled about it under his arm.

The judge of duels looked along the shoreline in the direction the three boats had gone. He had accompanied the surgeon in his launch. Gallatin and Ke had used the boat of the Chinaman Mingren Yang. The captain and Cochran had crossed the bay in the captain's gig. All the crews with their boats had been promptly directed to go around the coast of the island until they were out of sight of the dueling place.

Angel Island was a military reservation. An army post was located a mile away on the opposite end of the island. The soldiers should not be able to hear the shots and come to interfere. This duel would occur as planned.

The judge had fought many duels. There were dozens of scars on his body and dead men behind him to prove it. He knew the Code Duello and its twenty-six commandments better than any man in San Francisco. That was why the angry men came to him to be judge of duels. Even for killing there should be rules.

Still he was growing tired of all the bloodshed. He believed old men, as they approached their own deaths, knew that life was quite precious.

Tom Gallatin noticed the judge check his

watch and then bundle himself back in his cape. There was more time to wait. He turned to look up over the hill. The wind moaned a dirge as it came through the low scrub brush and boulders. Mist lay like patches of smoke in the eroded hollows just above him. He felt the wetness, so unlike the eastern desert country where he was born and raised.

He glanced around at his opponent. Captain Douchane had brought his ship through the Golden Gate three days before. Her main cargo had been three hundred and thirty-two Chinamen from Canton, China, heading for the Gum Shan, the Golden Mountains of California, to find their fortune in gold. Soon after the Chinamen had climbed up from the crowded steerage deck quarters and unloaded, the tale of the deaths of forty-three of their comrades began to spread swiftly over the docks.

Mingren Yang, a wealthy merchant who outfitted newly arrived Chinamen for the goldfields, was Tom's employer. He had first told Tom of the rumor and asked him to investigate. Tom had gone to the dormitories in Chinatown where the foreign gold seekers from the *Sierra Wind* were temporarily housed.

He knew their language moderately well, for he had spent a winter with a group of Chinese miners digging for gold on the Snake River in Oregon. So the men answered willingly when he asked questions in their tongue. Some did not know of the deaths, stating it must have happened in a part of the ship different from where they had traveled. Others told Tom that once during the seven-thousand-mile journey from China, several men became ill of a stomach malady after eating foul food. They complained of the sickness and the ship's doctor came to examine them. He ordered those in the worst condition to be brought up on the top decks. They were never seen again. One of the men that Tom questioned said his sleeping space was near the hatchway to the main deck and that he had seen the white sailors throwing bodies overboard.

Tom had gone to the pier where the *Sierra Wind* was tied up. The captain and the ship's doctor had been polite at first. They informed Tom the port authorities had been there and had queried all the crew and officers and read the ship's log. No Chinamen were missing from the original number boarded in Canton, except for one who had died and was buried at sea. His death was properly recorded in the log. They could not account for the rumor of the dead Chinamen.

Douchane became quarrelsome at Tom's continued questioning. "What is all this to you? No Chinamen died, but for the one. And suppose there had been, they were just Chinamen. Now get off my ship."

Tom responded sharply. "There is more to this than what you say."

"Are you calling me a liar, you young ass?" retorted Douchane.

"Men have told me that some of the Chinamen on your ship died and their bodies were thrown overboard. Either they lied or you do. And why would they lie, for they had nothing to gain."

"If you were the age of a man, I would see you over the sights of my pistol," snarled the captain.

"I am more than old enough to meet you with guns," Tom threw the challenge back.

"Then so be it. Have your second meet with my first officer, Mr. Cochran. He can make the arrangements for me. I say tomorrow morning should be the time, for I must leave on the evening tide." The captain stomped off forward on the deck toward his cabin.

The judge checked his watch and walked to the center of the meadow. "It is time to commence," he called to the adversaries and their seconds.

The pairs of men came angling in. The surgeon drew close with his satchel of medical paraphernalia.

Both Douchane and Gallatin removed their coats and tossed them to the ground.

The judge spoke to the two duelists. "Is there any argument I can make to persuade you to forgo this contest?"

"No," responded Gallatin first.

"I also say no," said Douchane. He appeared relaxed.

The judge looked from the face of the captain, weathered and hardened by wind and salt water, to the youthful countenance of Gallatin. The captain seemed confident. He had fought six duels that the judge knew about, and he was still whole and hearty.

Gallatin was extremely young, probably not yet twenty. He had been in San Francisco about two months. The judge had seen him only once before, late one night in the Sailor's Joy Saloon on The Embarcadero. Gallatin had fought and killed a man named Keggler.

Gallatin had stopped a poker game when Keggler had covered a bet with a cube of gold nearly as large as a man's palm. He had accused Keggler of murdering his friends in Oregon and stealing the beautiful natural crystal of the yellow metal. When Keggler had reached for his six-gun, Gallatin had easily beaten him to the draw and shot him.

The same night, six comrades of Keggler were found slain on the docks, killed by sword and pistol. That deed was also laid at the feet of Gallatin. The tale told was that Gallatin had trailed Keggler and his band of thieves to San Francisco, hunted them down, and slew them every one.

"Allow me to see the weapons," said the judge.

Cochran and Ke removed the Colt revolvers from their respective boxes and holster and presented them to the judge.

The judge asked, "Shall one cartridge in each weapon suffice? In that way if a man misses his opponent, there shall be no second shot at him."

Again both men responded in the negative.

The judge flipped open the cylinders of the guns and examined the loads. "They are satisfactory," he said, closing the pistols and handing them to the duelists. "As previously agreed to by your seconds, the distance shall be fifteen paces by each of you. I ask you, shall the firing begin at my signal, my call, or at will?"

"At will," said Gallatin.

"We will do it as this fellow wants," said Douchane.

"Then stand before me and face in opposite directions. Go fifteen paces and halt. When I call turn, you may then turn about and fire as you will it.

"Stand ready. But I caution you, do not fire until I give the word."

The judge paused, then directed. "Go fifteen paces."

The duelists stepped out over the grass from each other. The surgeon and the two seconds moved off to the beach. The judge backed away from the line of fire.

The duelists finished their last stride. They stood motionless as the rocks on the hillside. A deep hush held sway upon the meadow.

The raucous call of an early hunting seabird ravaged the silence of the morning. The white bird sailed past, its head turned downward and its black eyes evaluating the gathering of men.

Tom listened for the voice of the judge and gazed out over the bay to the coastal hills where lay the broad spread of structures that made San Francisco. He heard the water lapping leisurely against the grainy sand of the beach. Men did absurd things to repay old debts, he thought.

"Turn!" snapped the judge's tense voice.

Tom spun around, his hand lifting the six-gun. As the weapon rose, his thumb cocked the hammer and his finger tightened on the trigger. The pistol came level, partially extended in front of him. He fired.

Douchane staggered at the punch of the bullet. He was hit. The damn fellow was amazingly fast. But there was no pain. So not a bad wound.

Douchane tried to complete the raising of his pistol. It was terribly heavy. He began to lean to the side toward the bay. He caught a glimpse of his ship as he toppled. His face plowed into the grass of the meadow.

For a handful of seconds, all the men remained motionless. Then the surgeon and Cochran broke from their trance and ran to kneel at Douchane's still form.

After a moment the surgeon removed his hands from the body. He shook his head. "It is done. He is dead."

The judge turned away and walked down to the shoreline. He shivered inside his cape. He wanted to be quickly gone from this killing place. He cast a look in the direction the boats had gone. The crews had been told to return speedily at the sound of gunfire.

Gallatin retrieved his coat and tugged it on. He cast his view on the body of the sea captain and thought of Sigh Ho, a man he had known far away in the Oregon country. My friend Ho, you are dead, but hear me. You saved my life when I was shot and would have surely died. In repayment I took revenge upon those men who slew you. Now I have killed this man Douchane for poisoning some of your people. You and I are today even. Nothing more is due.

Tom went to the water's edge. He felt a release from owing a very heavy debt and a sadness at having killed again.

The judge glanced at the young man's face, hard as granite. The sea captain had been outrageously outclassed. Gallatin had spun about and made the fastest draw the judge had ever witnessed. His pistol had flamed before the captain could raise his weapon. The duel had been more of an execution than a contest.

The three boats came into view. The oarsmen were rowing strongly, a race without either crew mentioning it. As they drew nearer they saw Gallatin by the water and the body in the meadow. The boats slowed and pulled together. Money passed from the captain's gig to Gallatin's launch.

"Bring the captain's boat in close to the beach so we can place his body aboard," called the judge.

Chapter 2

San Francisco was a city built on sand hills adjacent to a wide bay. A broad avenue, The Embarcadero, paralleled the shore for nearly a mile. Many streets ran directly west from the beachfront and up the steep grade of the hills.

Several rackety wooden piers extended hundreds of feet out into the bay east of The Embarcadero. The longest was the quarter-mile-long Meig's Lumber Wharf, always loaded to overflowing with mounds of boards, planks and beams needed to build the great city. More than twoscore ships, both steam and sail and of various sizes, were berthed at the docks.

The launch transporting Tom and Ke from the duel on Angel Island tied up at the shore end of the northernmost pier. The two men climbed onto the pier. The dueling judge and the surgeon were docking nearby. Both groups nodded a silent farewell to each other.

"Tom, we should report to Mingren Yang as soon as possible and tell him what has happened and that you are safe," said Ke. "He will be waiting our word anxiously."

"We can go there straightaway," replied Tom. Tan Ke was Mingren Yang's lieutenant and entrusted with many duties.

"Then let us hurry," said Ke. Yang demanded to be informed immediately of events that might affect his vast holdings.

They strode off along the wharf that was jammed with horse-drawn drays, wagons and carts. Stevedores carried heavy loads up and down the gangways of several ships. Seamen, ship's officers, craftsmen and travelers hustled about speaking a Babel's tongue of languages. A thumping, steam-powered pile driver was hammering long timbers into the bottom of the bay to lengthen the pier. A chuffing steam paddy added its hiss and clank as it hauled sand from along the pier to deepen the water so the larger ships could come closer in to the land.

Tom relaxed from the tension-filled time of the duel and watched the bustle of the rich and thriving city. San Francisco had one of the best natural harbors in the world. Ships sailed from here to every major seaport of all the faraway continents in the world. The city was connected to the inland commerce of the United States by the transcontinental railroad completed in the spring of 1869, a year past. Its terminus was Sacramento. Constant riverboat and barge traffic on the Sacramento River completed the spanning of the continent from sea to sea.

The population was estimated at one hundred and sixty thousand people. Thirty thousand of that number were Chinese. Many other nationalities were also represented in large numbers. The city was growing rapidly.

Tom and Ke left the docks and the blocks of warehouses, large and cavernous and crowding close to the beach. They turned onto Market Street and began to climb its steep grade. Soon they had passed Harpenning Block and the four-story Grand Hotel with its four hundred rooms, and entered a section of smaller businesses intermixed with residential structures.

They walked along Market Street for a few minutes and then veered right on Dupont Street. Six blocks later, they came to a two-story building of a large size, occupying half a block. A sign, extending out from the building and over-hanging the sidewalk, read CHINESE FOODS, MINGREN YANG, PROPRIETOR. The sign was very new.

The structure was surrounded by buildings of like age and character. All were badly in need of paint. Tom knew the dilapidated exterior was deliberately maintained so that the white people of the town would not become jealous of the Chinaman's growing wealth. A bell tinkled as Tom and Ke entered the door.

A young man was seated at a low counter. Behind him were long series of shelves reaching to the ceiling and chock-full of a multitude of varieties of dry goods and foodstuffs, extending rearward into the dark recesses of the store.

A second Chinaman at a table on the right near the wall sprang up as Tom and Ke entered. "Hello, Ke, Tom," he said.

Both men nodded a return greeting and continued along one of the aisles between the shelving and out a door in the rear. The room was quite large. Four men were at desks calculating numbers from sheets of paper on abacus boards and recording sums in ledgers. Beyond them, three men were unpacking items from large wooden crates and repackaging various portions of the contents into heavy burlap bags of a size a man could easily carry.

Two men sat at a table near a barred door and played dominoes. They immediately came to their feet when they saw Ke.

He made a slight gesture and the men reseated themselves. Tom and Ke passed by and went through another door.

The room was splendidly decorated with long silk drapes on the walls. Thick mohair carpets covered the floor. The finest wooden furniture, delicate and ornately carved, was arranged in a most pleasing pattern.

Mingren Yang's voice reached them from a shadowy corner of the room. "I have been waiting, Tom. It is good to see you. Are you unhurt?"

"Yes, Mr. Yang," Tom replied.

Yang arose from an overstuffed chair and came forward. He was dressed in richly embroidered silk mandarin pants and blouse. He evaluated Tom with quick, alert eyes.

"I assume neither of you have eaten," said Yang. "I have had food prepared. Let us go and refresh ourselves with a delicious breakfast and talk." He led the way from the room.

Ke described the duel to Yang. The merchant sat quietly for a moment, thoughtfully rotating his tiny cup of black tea on the top of the table. He looked at Tom. "You may feel some remorse at having killed this sea captain. However, I feel confident that he did, through trying to reduce costs and make his voyage more profitable, feed spoiled or contaminated food to part of his passengers and they died.

"I regret you and Douchane had angry words and you had to fight him. Still the authorities were obviously not going to pursue the incident. It has been the law since 1854 that Chinamen could not testify against white men. Justice was not going to be had by the families of the dead men. Perhaps some form of repayment for a wrongful deed has now been had through your effort. I believe Quan Ing would be pleased."

Tom felt sorrow that Quan Ing, the venerable Chinese merchant, was not alive and still ruling his financial domain with his calm and gentle patience. But the aged Ing had died with no heirs. Mingren Yang, the trusted lieutenant, had assumed total control.

Quan Ing had already reached middle age when he arrived in San Francisco in 1850 with the first large wave of Chinese gold miners. An intelligent man, he determined wealth lay in the city and not in the search for gold in the mountains. Starting frugally with a small handful of gold, he had built a financial empire of three clipper ships, a warehouse and several barracks. He transported cargo and Chinamen from Canton and other Chinese ports to San Francisco. He could house one thousand of his sojourning countrymen at a time and outfit them for their journey to the mountains. Nearly all of them were uneducated farmers who spoke no English so Ing freely aided them in their dealings with the Americans.

Quan Ing had helped Tom take his revenge upon the thief Keggler and his gang of murderers for killing Sigh Ho and his entire crew of thirty-one miners on the Snake River in Oregon. During that battle with Keggler, Tom had grown to respect the aged Chinaman and had accepted an offer of employment as a guard from him. Within a month, Ing became ill and died. Tom had stayed on to work for Mingren Yang for the past two months.

Where Ing had been small, studious and quiet, Yang was muscular and energetic. Tom had seen Yang in the weapons training room in the basement of the building with his Chinese guards, performing mock battles with a knife. He was very skilled and amazingly quick.

Tom had seen Yang in a true fight, fierce and deadly. It had happened the first night when Tom had arrived in San Francisco. After supper with Ing, Tom had gone for a walk about the town. Three shanghaiers had attacked him in the night, planning to knock him unconscious and sell him to an outbound ship as a crewman. Yang had come out of the darkness to help Tom fight the men. The Chinaman had easily killed one of the crimps with his knife, while Tom slew the others. Tom learned afterward that Ing had sent Yang to help keep him safe in a strange and violent city.

Ing had always forbidden his men to use firearms. Yang had immediately removed that taboo upon Ing's death. Now the guards had been intensively practicing with pistols. They were becoming very expert with the new weapons.

Tom had heard rumors that Yang had expanded Ing's business to transporting slave girls and opium. He had seen no evidence of that and hoped it was not true.

Tom spoke. "It has been less than a year that I came off the Alvord Desert of Oregon. I did not know men before that, only my father. He told me that I might have to fight men who would take what was not theirs. I have met some of those men and I have killed them. He told me also not to get to like killing. I do not."

"Sometimes the only justice in the world is a man's own strong arm," said Yang.

"I believe you are correct. But I want no more of it," responded Tom. He was tired after the strain of the duel. "Will you be needing me the rest of the day?"

"No. The day is yours to do with as you like. Tomorrow, go early to the warehouse on the docks. There will be a load of new arrivals from China, nearly two hundred. Ke will be there. I wish for you to escort them from the docks to the dormitories on Stockton Street. A gang of unemployed white men beat up some Chinamen this morning on The Embarcadero. I am afraid the violence will become worse."

"I will see Ke at daybreak," said Tom. He arose and walked from the room. The conflict between the Chinamen and white workers was becoming more vicious. The white men often attacked the arriving foreigners on the streets, usually after they had passed the customs station of the port authorities. Tomorrow would be a hard and dangerous day.

Ke closed the door behind Tom. He reseated himself and spoke to Yang. "The captain of the

Sierra Wind never had a chance to beat Tom. He was dead before he could lift his pistol."

Yang smiled. "Our young white friend is like a fierce hunting hawk. He is very capable of killing when he believes he is in the right. He has the fast gun to do it.

"We have enemies, white and Chinese, who with cunning and force are deadly competitors. Today we taught one of our white enemies a powerful lesson. That load of Canton men on the *Sierra Wind* was ours until the representative of the white man underbid us for their passage across the ocean. He will not so readily steal another cargo. And he must now find a captain for his ship."

"With Tom as our white soldier we can fight our white foes. But how did you know Tom and Douchane would fight?" asked Ke.

"I did not for certain. But I knew both men were quick to anger. Tom truly believes forty-three Chinese died of food poisoning on the *Sierra Wind*. Those of our people from that ship you hired to tell the tale were very convincing."

"Tom believes that what he sees and hears is the truth, the reality of things."

Yang's countenance turned thoughtful.

"For now he feels indebted to our countryman Sigh Ho. Sigh, by saving Tom's life, has made him feel he must help us, even against other white men. Soon I will increase his pay and determine if he will do our bidding for money."

"Though he is inexperienced in the world, he has a keen mind," said Ke. "He also speaks our language sufficiently well to communicate with our people. One day he may discover what ruse we have played on him. His anger and skill with the gun could be turned against us."

"That is very true," said Yang. "So we must always know what he is thinking and doing. I have taken steps to insure we find out those things. One of our women has gone to him. She will report back to us."

"We may have to kill him one day," Ke said.

"I think so, too. However, killing him must be only a last resort. I would prefer to have him shanghaied and sent on a very long journey on one of our competitors' ships. He would cause much trouble for them before they put him to death."

Tom walked down the long hall and climbed the stairs to his room, one among many on the second floor. He spread his blanket on the bed and began to pile his belongings on it. Now was the time to leave Yang's establishment and find lodging someplace less crowded and the doors unguarded and unlocked.

He often wondered how many rooms were in the giant building and the number of people that resided here. There must be twenty or so rooms and perhaps twice that many people. He could sense the dense presence of them. They did not seem to require much space in which to live.

He eyed the meager pile of his possessions on the blanket and grinned ruefully. He certainly did not own many worldly goods. However, Yang paid well and in time Tom could accumulate money. Also, he still had sixty ounces of gold he had mined on the Snake River of Oregon and had brought with him.

A soft knock sounded on the door. He turned, letting his hand fall near the six-gun at his side. After the duel this morning, he might have enemies among Douchane's friends. Tom did not believe any could get through Yang's guards. For just a moment, Tom reflected upon his decision to leave. There was safety here. Then he shrugged. There was also confinement and crowding. He would move out as he planned.

"Come in," Tom said in Chinese.

A young woman dressed in dark blue silk entered and bowed very low. "I am Chun Zheng," she said in a pleasant voice.

Tom studied the small female as he waited for her to state what she wanted. She was exceedingly lovely. Her skin was like a dark shade of perfect ivory. She had that allure that made a man want to reach out and touch her.

She remained standing motionless, her head lowered. Tom realized she was not going to add to her first statement.

"What is it you want?" he asked.

"I am Chun Zheng," she repeated. Her tone implied he should understand what her name meant. She did not look up.

"So tell me why you are here."

"Did not Honorable Yang tell you? He has sent me. I am yours to do with as you desire."

"Look at me when I talk to you," directed Tom, suddenly aggravated at Yang for taking it upon himself to send the girl.

Her large black eyes flashed up to meet his. "I did not intend to anger you."

There was a tinge of fear in her voice. Tom did not like to see that.

"Where did you come from?"

"Oh. There are many of us. We wait for Honorable Yang to decide what to do with us."

"There are many of you? How many? Where?"

"He selected eight of us to come and live here in this big house. A much larger group of girls is in another house in the city. I do not know where that is."

"You are waiting for husbands?"

"That would be nice." There was a doubtful expression on her face.

Tom stepped forward and reached out to touch the smooth cheek of the girl. She flinched at the contact. Then she smiled quickly to cover her involuntary movement.

"You do not want to be here with me?"

"Honorable Yang has instructed me to come here. Therefore, I am pleased to be here."

"Go back to where you were," said Tom quietly.

"But I now have the room next to yours." She pointed at the wall on his left.

"You are very pretty, but I do not want you here."

Fear widened her eyes and her hands came together in front to grasp each other tightly. "But you must like me and want me. Honorable Yang will be angry and he will punish me."

"I am leaving this house," said Tom. He gestured at his possessions on the blanket. "See. I am already packed to go. Yang will not punish you for something I caused."

"If you go, then I shall go with you. I believe Honorable Yang would wish that."

"No. Go and wait for a Chinese man for a husband. There are many bachelors in San Francisco."

"Why do you dislike me?"

"I do not dislike you. I have other plans and they do not include a woman. Now please leave me."

"If you make me go, Honorable Yang will think I am at fault. He will sell me and they will put me in one of the cribs the women talk about. I shall be made a whore."

"Yang would not do that. You say that to make me change my mind. But I will not. Now go."

She started to say something, then caught herself. She bowed very low. Her small, slippered feet whispered on the carpet as she departed.

"Damnation!" said Tom out loud. He stood looking at the closed door. She was sent to him by Yang as a present. As if she were a thing, a piece of property that could be owned and done with as it pleased a person. He shook his head angrily.

Tom rolled his belongings in the blanket and tied it with a rough jerk. He fretted about what Chun had said, that there were other girls waiting. His step was heavy as he descended the stairs and went along the hall to an outside door. He felt more strongly than ever that he must get away from Yang's establishment.

The guard let him out without comment, though he registered some surprise at the blanketed bundle under Tom's arm. Immediately after the bolt of the door was rammed home in its locking socket, Tom heard the thud of feet as the guard hurried off through the house. Tomorrow might be a little rough when he explained to Yang why he had left.

After an hour of searching, Tom found a clean apartment of one large room on Mason Street near Sutter. The lodging was on the ground floor in the front of a large private dwelling. He paid for a month's rent and carried his possessions inside.

He had not slept well during the night and he lay down on the bed with a sigh. He lay awake for several minutes before sleep would come.

Chapter 3

The river ferry bound from Sacramento to San Francisco passed Point San Pablo and entered the salt water of San Francisco Bay. The ferry veered to a course due south and a few minutes later Angel Island slid past on the starboard side. The captain sounded a blast on the steam whistle to announce his imminent arrival at the docks of the city.

The tide was flooding into the bay. The current swirled around the canting masts and spars sticking up above the water from scores of dead ships, abandoned by gold-crazy men and now sunken at their anchors and forgotten on the bottom of the bay. The captain steered a course among the wrecks along a passageway that had been created by the port authorities by dragging aside the rotting hulks.

The broad harbor lay in full view to Luke Coldiron from his location on the top deck of the riverboat. The water of the bay had a red sheen from the crimson sun settling close to the western horizon.

He counted forty-six ships at anchor and motionless on the red water. Nearly as many vessels were tied up at the rickety-looking piers. A host of men and vehicles were scurrying about on the wharfs and the wide The Embarcadero transporting a huge tonnage of cargo to and from the ships.

The broad-beamed river ferry slowed and coasted in to its berth. The paddle wheel reversed its rotation, the water boiled and the boat gently nudged the wooden pilings. Lines were made fast to cleats on the dock.

"All passengers disembark," called the deck steward. He moved to help two seamen swing out the top deck gangway and lower it to rest one end on the wharf. A strong ramp was run out from the lower deck to accommodate the several dozen horse-drawn wagons and buggies and saddle mounts that had been transported.

Coldiron took his duffel bag and walked to the side railing where he could see the dock. In the duffel bag were twenty-five thousand dollars in gold and paper money. He had come to San Francisco to play poker and to visit a longtime friend.

He stood patiently in the cool wind coming off the bay. He was a lean man and tall, not old not young, a man seasoned from many battles. His hair was black and hung down to the top of his shirt collar. It was pulled back and held in place by a broad-brimmed hat.

The passengers hastened down the gangway. There were city people, miners from the goldfields of the Sierra Nevada, loggers from the lumber camps, and farmers who tended the thousands of irrigated acres of cropland beside the river. However, most of the arrivals were part of the multitude of people flooding to the West on the new railroad from the Eastern states.

Coldiron hung back and was the last passenger to leave the riverboat. He walked leisurely along the dock, avoiding the working men. He stopped for a minute to view a hissing steam winch hoisting a cargo net of freight from the hold of a ship and then depositing it on the pier. Most of the cargo of the ships was being moved by burly white stevedores. However, at one vessel a line of small brown Chinamen, carrying loads on their backs larger than they were, filed up and down the gangway.

Coldiron left the docks and crossed The Embarcadero. He walked up Market Street, often glancing both ways along the thoroughfares to view the large buildings and the crowds of people and vehicles. There was a constant rumble of noise all around him from the iron-rimmed wheels of the conveyances and shod hooves of the horses passing on the wooden planking that surfaced the street.

He wondered about the great quantity of lumber needed to cover the street until he recalled the huge forests on the coast of northern California and Oregon. With water transportation timbers could be brought cheaply to San Francisco.

He turned north on Montgomery Street. The nature of the businesses changed abruptly. Saloons, billiard halls and card rooms dominated the blocks. Five pretty young women sat in swings on the porch of a house. They spoke and smiled at Luke.

The sun was sinking and long shadows were growing in the streets. It was time to end his inspection of San Francisco for the day, and find Major Whittiker's residence.

Three white men stood leaning against the brick front of a billiard hall. Coldiron veered aside to stop near them.

He spoke to the group. "I'm looking for Hyde Street. Can either of you fellows tell me how to get there?"

"Why do you want to go to Hyde?" asked a heavy-muscled redheaded man.

"That's not important. Do you know where it is?"

"Sure, but I don't see any need to tell you," said the redhead. He looked at his comrades and winked.

"How about one of you other two. Can you tell me how to reach Hyde Street?"

The redhead pushed away from the wall and folded his big fists. "Mister, I do the talking for all three of us. You tell me why you want to go to Hyde and maybe I'll tell you how to get there."

The other two men grinned broadly. They liked these games with strangers.

Coldiron laughed, a brittle sound. The bully-boys wanted to start a fight with someone new to San Francisco. But not tonight, thought Coldiron, he was here only for pleasure.

"Well, thanks for nothing," said Coldiron. He turned to step away from the men and proceed along the street.

"Don't be a smart aleck with me," growled the redhead. He moved swiftly forward, his hand darting out to catch Coldiron by the shoulder.

Coldiron pivoted aside to wrench free. He flipped the tail of his coat out of the way and drew his six-gun with a flick of his wrist. He struck a short, savage blow with the gun on the man's outstretched hand. He felt the bones shatter as the heavy iron weapon slashed down.

The man cried out in sudden pain and pulled the mangled hand against his chest, to cuddle it there.

Coldiron laughed his brittle laugh again. He glanced at the other two men. They did not move.

Luke pointed the pistol at the center of the wounded man's nose. "Since we've now started a good conversation, you tell me where Hyde Street is or I'm going to play games with your face."

The man swallowed, his Adam's apple pumping up and down. "Up there, up the hill to the west. Just another five blocks or so. It runs north and south."

"I thought you might know about Hyde Street," said Coldiron. "By the way, if you've lied to me, I'll come right back here to see you."

He swept his sight at the other men. "You two are with him, so that means I'd be looking for you, too. Is there any correction you want to make in what he said? I'll get mad if I walk in the wrong direction."

One of them spoke hastily. "No. He told you the right way."

"Good," said Coldiron. "Since you vouch for him, I'll go that way." He walked off.

Sam Whittiker's residence was a massive two-story wooden house with elaborate gingerbread trim and all painted a light shade of yellow. It was located in a section of the city with many other homes of equal or more pretentious dimensions. Obviously the rich man's section of San Francisco.

Luke had known Sam Whittiker in 1863 and '64. Whittiker had been a major in the Union Army and commander of the army garrison at Santa Fe. Luke had sold him several hundred head of saddle mounts for the cavalrymen stationed at the post. Whittiker had been an excellent officer.

Whittiker had left the Army five years ago at the end of the Civil War. He had purchased a ferry and put it on the Sacramento to San Francisco run. Then he had added a second and a third. It appeared Sam was accumulating wealth.

Luke lifted the iron knocker and rapped on the solid oak door. Almost immediately the portal swung open and a young Chinaman examined him for a moment and then bowed his head.

"My name is Luke Coldiron. Is Major Whittiker at home?"

"Yes, sir. Please come in."

Coldiron stepped into the vestibule. The Chinaman took his duffel and hat and coat.

"Who is it, Yee?" a woman's voice called. Emily Whittiker came into view across the spacious living room.

"Well, Luke Coldiron. We have been expecting you. Come in. Oh. Come in." She rushed forward and hugged him.

"Yee, Mr. Whittiker is in the stable. Run and bring him here. Tell him an old and dear friend has arrived." She laughed happily.

"Yes. At once, Mrs. Whittiker." The small man glided off.

"Sam will be very pleased you accepted his invitation to come to San Francisco. Luke, it is a marvelous city. We have excellent theaters, restaurants and stores. Traveling troupes of actors from all the larger American cities, and also London and Paris, come here to put on their plays. Anything that can be bought in Philadelphia or Boston can be bought here "

Luke heard footfalls and a man hurried from the rear of the house.

"Luke, damn glad to see you," said Whittiker. He thrust out his hand. Major Whittiker was of medium height and a straight-backed man with a square face. His military training was obvious. Luke liked the man.

"Hello, Sam," replied Luke, taking the proffered hand. "Thank you for your letter. I was getting tired of roping and branding horses."

"You must have done a lot of it, for I feel some damn thick calluses on your hands, awfully thick for a cardplayer."

"Only card sharks need soft hands."

Whittiker chuckled. "And you're not a shark? Let's go into the library and talk and have some bourbon. I remember you like that."

"I will see to the preparation of supper," said Emily. "You two go ahead. Sam, save part of the gossip for me. Luke, don't tell Sam anything until I have a chance to listen."

"Then what will we talk about now?" asked Sam.

"What Luke really came here for."

*   *   *

Relaxed in their longtime friendship, Luke and Sam sat quietly in soft, leather chairs and pulled at their drinks.

"When did you arrive?" asked Sam.

"Two or three hours ago. I walked around the town a little, just getting the feel of the city."

"Be cautious," said Sam. "There are robbers, ruffians and pickpockets in sections of the town. Carry your pistol at night, or when you go on the Barbary Coast, that's a stretch of Pacific, Kearney and Broadway. Also, be alert on The Embarcadero. Some of those ships at anchor are waiting for a crew. Crimps are working the streets and bars for strong men. They'll either dope them with a Mickey Finn or hit them over the head. Many of the ships sailing from San Francisco have shanghaied crew members."

"I've heard of that custom."

"Those are the obvious dangers. There are secret Chinese societies called tongs, with their *boo how doy*, hatchet men. They are as tough and mean as any white gang. Fortunately, they almost always fight among themselves for territory to extort protection money, sell opium and control the whores. They collect illegal money in a dozen ways. There are white men that are even worse. But we can talk about that later. Most people in San Francisco are honest men. What did you think of our city?"

Luke chuckled. "Well, it's a pretty city seeing it from the bay. And you have a beautiful view from here."

"Almost as pretty as your horse ranch in the Sangre de Cristo Mountains of Colorado," said Whittiker.

"Nearly," smiled Luke. Nothing could match the wild beauty of Gachupin Canyon on the drainage of the Vermejo River. He had been gone from there only eight days and already he felt the loneliness for it creeping in. It was good to know where you wanted to live your life and even to die when you became a very old man.

He had discovered the valley twenty-seven years before while transporting his catch of beaver pelts from the towering Sangre de Cristos to Santa Fe. More than a thousand wild horses had been grazing the meadows, far more than the land could feed. Many were thin and stunted. He found scores of skeletons and decaying carcasses of horses that had died of starvation during the winter. Yet Luke recognized the huge potential of the mountain valley to produce excellent horses.

A month later he returned from Santa Fe with two packhorses straining under heavy burdens of powder and shot. During that first summer, he slew more than eight hundred horses; those that were sick, lame or had poor body form, and almost all of the stallions. So many animals were slain that the coyotes and wolves stopped hunting, merely following the killer human and growing fat eating the choicest tidbits from the carcasses left at his ambushes.

Out of all that great herd he allowed only two hundred mustangs to live, the start of his famous Steel Trap Brand. Still today additional horses, throwbacks, mutants or those undesirable for any reason, were destroyed to continually improve the herd.

Whittiker went to a big oak desk and from a

drawer extracted a box of cigars. Luke accepted one of the offered tobaccos, ran it past his nose to savor the pungent aroma, and struck a match.

As he brought the flame to the end of the cigar, the chair in which he sat began to sway. The floor shifted. A tall candlestick toppled off a table. The walls creaked and a crack ran across one of the panes in a window.

Then the floor and walls became firm and quiet. The chandelier hanging in the center of the room continued to swing gently.

"What in the hell was that?" questioned Luke.

"An earth tremor," said Sam. He arose and replaced the candlestick in its original position. "I must get a glazier and have that window repaired tomorrow."

Sam glanced at Luke holding the now dead match. "These small earthquakes happen several times each year. They are not destructive, but are hard to get used to."

"I have heard they can be dangerous," Luke said.

"The stronger ones surely can. The Indians that once lived here had a legend. It described how the earth shook and the ocean was tossed into a giant storm of waves taller than the height of five men. A village on the beach was washed into the sea with many people killed. The Mexicans that have been here longer than we Americans also tell of earthquakes, but none as powerful as the one of the Indians' legend."

Sam handed Luke another match and continued to speak. "I have seen a moderate earthquake. It was a year and a half ago, October of 1868. I was on the street. The ground rolled like waves and every few seconds it would joggle up and down. There was a heavy grinding noise. Horses were rearing and some tried to run, but were knocked to the ground.

"A crack of a few yards' length gaped a foot wide in the street and then was instantly jammed back shut. The force of the closure was so strong that a ridge of dirt like a long narrow grave remained where the fissure had been. Every door of every house was pouring people. That is the safest place to go, out of the buildings and into the street where the walls or brick and stone don't fall on you."

Luke considered the immense power that would be required to move the town, indeed to shake the very earth and sea. "What causes the earthquakes?" he asked.

"We are sitting right on top of what geologists say is one of the largest faults in the world. The two walls of the fault sometimes move past each other. When that happens, an earthquake occurs and things get shaken around."

"I see," said Luke. He lit the match and drew on his cigar.

"Emily instructed me to be certain you stayed here with us, so don't disappoint her and me," said Whittiker, dismissing the earth movement.

"That's nice of her. And I accept with pleasure."

"Good." Whittiker settled back and examined Coldiron through the gray stringers of smoke that rose from their cigars. "You have one of the biggest ranchos in both Colorado and New Mexico, and without doubt the finest horses even including those from the ranches in Texas and Mexico. You are a savvy businessman. So why travel all the way to San Francisco for a poker game with strangers?"

Coldiron's eyes, emotionless like water, rested upon Whittiker as he pondered the question.

Whittiker sensed, as he had many times in the past, the intelligence of the man's mind, and he had witnessed the incisive, oftentimes violent primitiveness of Luke's approach to handling a problem. It was told Luke had killed more than twenty-five men, anyone who dared to steal even one of his horses, or intrude upon his land in an unfriendly manner.

Whittiker knew Coldiron made an excellent friend and a very terrible enemy. He had one great weakness, playing poker for high stakes.

"I wanted to see you and Emily," said Luke. "Also, to visit the fastest-growing city in America. I've been told its people are the most lively and daring. That it is the place for a man who likes a fast game of cards. Now tell me what you have arranged for me."

"I passed the word of your coming to California to visit and desiring a game of poker. Several men wanted to play you. Some were professional gamblers. I thought you would prefer to play with businessmen.

"I have four of the city's best poker players. There is André Beaulieu, a sour-faced Frenchman. A shrewd man, owns five clipper ships. Transports Chinese men who want to be gold miners. Smuggles opium and slave girls.

"Jeremiah Trenton is a state senator. He wants to be U.S. senator. Youngish fellow. Sharp mind.

"Albert McCubbin owns a lumber pier and several lumber mills on the north coast.

"Dan Tarter is an ex-army officer from the South. Just barely endures me since I was in the Union Army. He owns two ferries and some warehouses. Damn fine cardplayers.

"The men have been waiting for you to get here. The tale of your closing all four of the poker tables in the Elephant Corral Saloon in Denver in '64 is well known here. Also, we heard you took Ed Chase's bankroll. He once worked San Francisco before he migrated to Colorado and people still remember him here."

"That was a lovely two days of cardplaying," Luke said with a grin of remembrance.

"Your opponents here are all wealthy men. They are tough and don't like to lose, and they rarely do. You'll have a rough run for all that money."

"Will there be a professional dealer or will the deal rotate?"

"Rotates among the players."

"That gives them all the temptation to cheat."

"Because of your reputation, I think every one of them would be tempted to cheat. Some will think it perfectly all right to do so. All would like to see you have to borrow money to pay your passage home."

Coldiron laughed, his eyes dancing. "Two games going at one time. The natural fall of the cards and the fall when someone tries to add a little false luck to his hand."

Then his face became frosty. "That could get a man killed. But, Sam, you certainly organized an interesting game for your old friend. When can we start?"

"They were all in town as of yesterday. How about 1 P.M. tomorrow afternoon?"

"Fine. Now tell me what business schemes you have."

"The city needs a new pier and I am studying the water depths in the bay now to determine the feasibility of building one."

Luke nodded. "I saw the hustle and congestion of the men and vehicles on the docks, and that the men were working late in the evening. Also, there were a large number of ships anchored in the bay. I assume most of them were waiting for space to tie up. Do you have the location selected for your pier?"

"The best location with the deepest water close in to the shore has been taken." Sam went to his desk and shuffled through a stack of papers. He sorted out a map and spread it on the floor in front of Luke.

"This shows the water depth and the existing wharfs. It was prepared by the U.S. Navy about eight years ago and is the official map for navigation. See how shallow the water is. Over most of the bay it is less than thirty feet deep. Near the shore it is very shallow.

"Some of the depths of water off The Embarcadero at the time of the original construction of the piers were as great as twenty feet. Plenty deep for any ship at the time. Now some of the owners of the piers are having to dredge. It costs eight to ten cents a cubic yard to dredge and haul the sand and silt away. A fortune is being spent to keep the water deep enough for the larger ships. And the new ships are requiring an even greater depth of water, especially the steamships."

"Something is now different?"

Whittiker smiled broadly. "This must never go beyond you and me. One day I was on the northernmost pier. I saw a Chinaman fishing from a small skiff. He had anchored just here." Whittiker touched the map. "That's about eighty or a hundred feet north of the existing pier. When the Chinaman got ready to leave, he pulled his skiff up over his anchor and then lifted it up. He dragged in at least fifteen feet of line. This map shows that water depth was ten feet eight years ago."

Whittiker hesitated and regarded Coldiron. "Since the map was prepared, the water has become five feet deeper. The existing piers have changed the current of the tide and now it is scouring away the bottom of this location."

"So a pier built there would not require dredging," said Luke. "Damn clever idea."

"I will build a pier much stronger than any existing here now. It will have two winches, with boom arms, on a track so they can move from ship to ship. Perhaps you might want to be my partner?"

"I'll surely consider that."

Chapter 4

The schooner *Cloud Racer* reached the coast of California off San Francisco in the dusk of late evening. The captain ordered the sails lowered and halted the voyage. He had been under way for three months and had traveled seven thousand miles.

A sea anchor, a large funnel-shaped canvas object, nine feet at its greatest diameter, was lowered from the bow into the water at the end of two hundred feet of stout cable. The sea anchor would sink into the deep water and hold the schooner against the push of the wind. The vessel would drift not more than a mile during the night.

Zaishing Mo, The Keeper the women called him, stood on the deck of the schooner and stared at the distant shoreline of hills growing dim as the dusk deepened. He had a dangerous problem to resolve within the next few hours.

The white man, Black Drummond, had commissioned him to go to Canton, China, and purchase eighty young and beautiful virgins. That had been speedily accomplished after he arrived, requiring only three weeks of searching and posting of notices. The task had been made easy because a great storm had blown in off the South China Sea and destroyed wide sections of the coastal plains of Kwangtung Province. Thousands of people were homeless and starving. Many daughters were for sale, the money to be used for the survival of the family. The price had been most reasonable, an average cost of only three hundred dollars in gold.

He had assembled the women on the pier at Canton and placed them aboard a fast junk. The voyage down the Pearl River was swift, the river and the wind flowing in exactly the same direction. A rare event. The Gods had held them steady, uneasy partners to hurry The Keeper's journey.

The junk tied up to the side of *Cloud Racer* at anchor near Lintin Island in the mouth of the Pearl River. The girls were brought aboard and taken to their compartments in the forward part of the ship. The remainder of the cargo had already been loaded, tons of freight and two hundred men crowded into an impossibly cramped space in steerage. They were bound for America to dig a fortune from the Gum Shan, the Golden Mountains of California.

The sea was not gentle like the Pearl River. The wind gusted and screeched through the rigging of the schooner as it plowed east. The wind had come a very long distance and had pounded the surface of the ocean into waves of giant proportions. That did not bother The Keeper, for he never became seasick no matter how much a ship rolled and pitched.

He began to patrol the deck surrounding the quarters of the women. He wore a short sword at his side. There might be sailors or men from steerage who would come to make love to the virgins under The Keeper's protection.

He opened the hatchway of each compartment and stepped inside to check the condition of his charges. They were a miserable group of wretches, vomiting and moaning, or lying with stricken eyes and sallow face. All but one.

Ging Ti had glanced up from where she sat swaying effortlessly to the heave and plunge of the schooner. She smiled and bowed her head in greeting. This man was the agent for a rich merchant in America. She now belonged to that American.

The Keeper stared at Ging for several moments, evaluating her with a fresh eye. All the women were lovely, for he had selected them himself. But this one sat proud and strong among the others. A prize jewel among lesser jewels. Her gaze was open and direct, as if she were measuring him and the rest of the world against some internal standard. She was one of those women that men would gamble much to possess.

The virgins were forbidden to The Keeper even if he wanted to buy one. They were to be sold at a grand auction shortly after their arrival in San Francisco. Those men who would get the most beautiful of the virgins could well pay the magnificent sum of three thousand dollars. The least price expected was fifteen hundred dollars. His employer would reap a large fortune from this one venture.

That first night of the voyage, The Keeper came among the women of Ging's compartment and led her away to his cabin. There she fought him fiercely, for to be less than a virgin would mean a horrible unknown fate for her.

The Keeper beat her into submission. Later he returned her to the women's compartment. He warned her against telling anything to the other women. She crept into a corner and sat for hours. She did not cry.

The loveliness of Ging had stirred The Keeper to a complete disregard for the future. However, that future he had ignored would arrive before dawn. Black Drummond would come with his harbor boat before daylight and take the slave girls secretly into San Francisco. A doctor would examine the girls and Drummond would know what had happened on the voyage.

The Keeper was supposed to deliver eighty virgins. He had seventy-nine. His life was forfeit. If that was found out.

There was only one solution if The Keeper was to survive past tomorrow. It was better to hand over seventy-nine virgins rather than seventy-nine virgins and one girl who had been deflowered. Ging must vanish from the world of the living so her tale could never be told.

The decision made, The Keeper waited until all the decks became empty and the lights went out in the women's compartment. He waited some more, watching the moon rise. Then he went silently along the deck of the ship to the cabin where Ging slept.

She lay wide-eyed and uneasy as the night wore on. Tomorrow was a day to dread. What would her owner in America do with her now?

One of the girls tossed on her pallet and cried out. Ging jerked at the sound. Others had misgivings of the day to come. But never as much as Ging. She had been rendered valueless for the purpose she had been purchased. However, her father had the gold from her sale. No one could take that away from him.

Ging had been born the first of two girls, on her father's sailing junk out on the South China Sea. Her family spent practically all its time on that turbulent water. Her father was a fisherman, a skilled man who had made a suitable living for his wife and daughters.

The tossing deck of the junk was her play yard except during those short periods when they sailed to the city of Whampoa to sell their catch of ocean fish. She grew up independent, working hard at pulling the nets and wielding the sharp knife to clean the fish, sometimes very big creatures.

In those periods when the fishing was slow, but the wind good, her father would drag in all the nets, cram on as much sail as the single mast would carry, and they would run before the winds for miles. During those times, all would rest until near the end of the day when her mother would cook a special meal. Her father would dance with his three women, one after the other on the small central deck. The daughters felt this a grand honor and they loved him for his kindness.

He was a fierce man, fierce as only completely free men can be. He fought the storms that caught them on the sea and fought with his sharp knife the men on the docks when they tried to misuse one of his daughters.

The mighty typhoon trapped them tied to a wharf in the port of Whampoa. There was no warning so they could seek a protected harbor for the junk or run for the open sea, for even that was more desirable than being caught by the wind against an exposed shore.

The wind and waves beat the junk against the pier, shattered the stout wooden ribs and planking, and drowned the remains of the vessel. The family escaped with nothing, for all they had of value was the boat.

No—there was something else of value. The beautiful young daughter, Ging. They read the notices posted on the public bulletin boards. They saw the one stating the wish of Zaishing Mo to buy virgins.

Ging and the entire family walked the many miles from Whampoa to Canton. The Keeper evaluated Ging and was pleased by her beauty. The doctor examined her and a sale was made. The price agreed upon by her father was four hundred dollars in gold, one of the highest amounts paid. That quantity of precious yellow metal would buy another fishing junk, a vessel even better than the one her father had owned before. Some money would be left over for those times when the fish could not be found or they refused to be caught in the nets.

Ging felt moistness in her eyes as her mind recalled her father and mother and sister on the dock at Canton, raising their hands in final farewell. She knew she would never see them again.

Ging heard a key being cautiously inserted into the lock of the compartment door. The lock turned and the portal swung partway open.

The Keeper's hand slid inside and felt for her. He found her easily for he had ordered her to always sleep nearest the opening. He drew her outside.

"Make no sound," The Keeper hissed in a threatening voice.

Ging looked up at his flat face. It was evil and remorseless in the slanting rays of the moon. Oh, how she wished for her fish knife. She would gut this man with one fast, deep slice of the sharp blade.

"Come with me," ordered The Keeper. He led her across the dark deck to the rail at the edge of the ship.

Ging saw no one. But The Keeper always planned it that way. The other women in her compartment knew the man took her outside. They did not know more than that. They only suspicioned what happened. Ging understood in her young mind that this was one secret she must never disclose.

The Keeper pressed Ging against the wooden rail of the ship and his hands began to explore her body. Then he abruptly stopped.

His bony fist suddenly struck her in the pit of her stomach. She doubled over. Her breath escaped with an exploding, whistling sound. Instantly The Keeper hit her again, on the side of the head. She fell limply to the deck.

Ging could not catch her breath. Her lungs were rigidly locked and would not expand. Blackness filled her mind. She was still alive, but just barely.

The Keeper scooped her up and leaned over the side of the ship. He caught her by the hands and lowered her as far as he could reach. He released his hold. She dropped toward the black ocean.

Her body arrowed downward. The slender form plunged into the water, making no more sound than the splash of a fish.

The water was totally black, and frigid as the arctic glaciers from which it had come on the Alaskan Current. The cold shock of it bit to the marrow of her bones and tightened and stiffened her muscles with a wrench.

Ging sank rapidly, for her lungs held no air and provided no buoyancy. The water rushed past. Her dress washed up to catch on her arms and trailed and fluttered in her wake.

She had learned to swim before she could walk. That had been a requirement for survival for all the children of men who fished the stormy South China Sea. Now, without conscious thought, she tried to slow her rapid descent into the freezing, wet depths. The strokes of her hands were ineffectual, entangled and feeble in the dress.

The coldness cleared her mind. She peeled the dress off and let it loose. She reached out and fought the water, digging and grabbing at its slippery surface. Her fall toward the ocean bottom slowed and stopped.

She stroked and clawed upward through the dark depths for a great distance. The muscles and ribs of her chest quivered and ached to expand and suck in air, in a place where there was no air. She struggled to prevent the involuntary action. Many seconds passed and still the ascent did not end.

Stars began to burst in her head and pin-wheels of bright light were born and spun at an ever increasing speed. A black, cold numbness gathered around the periphery of her mind and pushed inward. Control of her body was slipping away from her grasp. Soon her lungs would open and the deadly salt water flood in.

Her outstretched arms broke the surface. Then her head popped free. The life-giving air rushed into her aching lungs. How delicious it was!

The murky bulk of the ship rode the gloom several body lengths distant. Ging turned her back to it and swam silently away on the waves. If The Keeper knew she was alive, he would use his sword to insure she died.

Most likely he had sealed her death the moment he dropped her from the ship. She was in extremely cold water, miles from the beach. Could she swim that distance in such frigid temperature?

The Keeper watched the water below him and listened sharply for sounds that would indicate Ging was alive. There was no sign of her. He turned and began to shout in English.

"One of the women has thrown herself overboard. Put some boats on the water quickly for we must save her."

Ging heard the cries from the ship, but could not understand the words. She swam more swiftly from the looming hulk of the schooner.

She had seen the orange ball of the moon rise over the land to the east just after sunset. She set a course toward it.

The rattling noise of blocks and tackle reached her as men swung out the small boats and lowered them. There were more shouts and she glanced back. Lantern lights bobbed on the water as boats cast off to seek her.

She faced back to the east. The moon was not a good guide, for it would change positions as the night passed. She located the polestar on her left side. Her father had pointed it out to her and told her how it never moved, hanging motionless in the heavens forever, a sailor's only true beacon when the sun hid behind the earth. She laid her head down in the water and began to swim.

Something brushed her leg. She recoiled, kicking away. Were there sharks in this American sea as there were in her China Sea?

The water thing did not touch her again. She made a hundred strokes and checked the polestar. Another hundred strokes. And another. She was so terribly cold.

You can make it, daughter of Wong Ti. Just keep reaching for the shore. She swam for a very long distance and then rolled to her back to rest. Her mind was becoming foggy and slow to act.

She heard her father calling her from far ahead. How did he get there? She rolled to her stomach and swam on and on toward him.

Ging believed she would have succeeded in making the land if the water had been her balmy South China Sea. But the cold of this foreign ocean had pierced her to the heart. Her arms were stiff, the muscles so chilled they had no strength and required a supreme effort to reach forward only a few inches. Her exhausted legs sank deeper and deeper in the water. She was foundering, she was finished.

Keeper, damn you to the wrath of all the Gods, I am going to die.

Some object, hard and solid, struck her on the head. She put out a hand to feel it. The thing was rough and had square corners. It was as wide as the length of her lower arm and a hand width in thickness. Holding on, she worked a course along it. The length was perhaps five times her height. It was a large wooden timber.

Ging raised herself partway up on the end of the plank. Splinters gouged her bare breast and chest. Her frozen flesh barely sensed the wounds. She kicked and squirmed to drag her body farther up on the flat, rough surface. Scores of the sharp slivers stabbed her.

With one last desperate yank she hitched herself mostly out of the water. She was totally spent. She lowered herself down on the tossing timber, wrapped her arms about the splintery object, and clutched it to her.

She let the black, cold numbness take her.

Chapter 5

Tom awoke in the afternoon, restless and disturbed by the killing in the duel. And by what Chun Zheng had said about Yang having other girls he was deciding what to do with. What kind of a situation was he getting involved in by working for Yang?

Taking his bedroll, he went toward the livery stable on Sutter Street. He needed a day away from the city and the crowds of people so he could think things out.

The black horse nickered a welcome to its master and nudged him playfully. Tom rubbed the long bony jaw. He had owned the fine horse for as long as he could remember. His father had given it to him as a small colt far away in the Oregon country.

Tom brushed the muscular body. He noted the gray hair invading the velvet charcoal coat. He felt sorrow at the aging of the animal. It was all he had from his youth and the only thing he cared about.

"You're getting old, you rascal," Tom told the cayuse. Getting a little soft, too, he thought.

The mount must be ridden more. That would be a pleasant chore.

Gallatin saddled, told the liveryman he would return on the morrow, and rode out. At a restaurant on Market Street, he had a lunch packed. Now prepared to spend the night under the May stars, he spoke to the black and it went willingly at a gallop up the sloping hill street between the rows of houses.

Four miles later, Tom reined the horse to a halt amid the brush on the top of Mount Sutro. He allowed the animal to catch its wind, then touched its flanks with his heels and began the long descent to the beach.

To the west, the crimson sun lay shimmering on the ocean. A tall-masted schooner with brilliant white sails was pinned against the darkening water. The ship, heading directly for the Golden Gate, raced swiftly on the wind, as if trying to reach an anchorage in San Francisco Bay before the darkness overtook it.

Upon reaching the shore, Tom removed the saddle from the black and slapped the animal away to graze. It liked his companionship and would not wander far.

Tom spread his bedroll on a patch of wild beach grass and laid out his supper. Idly he ate, listening to the break of the sea on the rock and sand.

A flock of shorebirds skimmed in to find their roost in the bushes before the night fell. They landed, uttered little chirping calls to each other, then became quiet.

He watched the ocean drown the sun. As the daylight whisked away into the sky and dusk came hurrying in, the sails of the ship dropped and the vessel became stationary on the rolling swells of the deep.

A cold wind began to blow off the water. Tom draped one of the blankets over his shoulders. He sat thoughtfully regarding the wet twilight settling on the ocean.

The big stars came out. A yellow moon rose over Mount Sutro and began to orb the earth. Tom crawled into his bedroll, propped his head on the saddle, and watched the stars begin their nightlong whirling turn across the ebony heavens.

He lay for a long time awake. He heard the tide's inexorable invasion of the land.

Unable to find sleep, he tossed aside his blankets and walked beside the water's edge. In the night's silver-blue moonglow, the brush, rock and beach grass held eerie shadowy forms. Tom felt the elemental sameness of the ocean shore to his desert.

A thumping sound reached him from ahead, something ramming against a rock in the border of the sea. He angled nearer to the waves sweeping in.

In the rays of moonlight streaking down, Tom saw a long, square sawn timber being raised by the incoming waves and then dropped upon a partially submerged boulder. He peered closer; a figure resembling a human form lay on the far end of the length of wood.

The timber struck more violently upon the rock and the figure stirred. The person's head rose a few inches and then fell back.

Tom lunged into the water. He caught his

breath at the arctic cold of the ocean. He waded hurriedly to the person's side.

A naked woman clutched the splintery wooden timber to her body. She moaned as Tom pried her hands loose. He lifted her and splashed to the shore. She was ice in his arms.

He ran with the woman to his camp and laid her on his blankets. In the flare of a match, he examined her for injuries. He found bruises and a hundred splinter wounds. Her breath was much too shallow and she was stiff with cold. She could die if not gotten warm quickly.

He was wet to his chest, shivering, and his teeth chattered. She was in much worse condition, too frozen even to shiver.

Tom thought of bundling her in the blankets and setting out immediately for San Francisco. But that was a distance of eight miles or more, at least an hour's ride at a gallop.

Swiftly he jerked off his sodden pants and shirt and lay down beside the woman. He wrapped the blankets tightly around them and took the woman in his arms. He pressed her to him and held her in the cold dark night.

Ging awoke and she was warm. A most wonderful sensation. The Keeper had failed to kill her. She had not drowned and the swim through the frigid water had ended. That added to the magnificent feeling. But where was she?

She opened her eyes to look about. A white man stared at her from a distance of a few inches. Their bodies were pressed tightly together and his arms were around her.

Her pulse raced with fright. Had she escaped one enemy only to fall into the hands of another? She tried to pull back from him, but a covering of some sort was wrapped about them, holding them face to face.

Tom saw the alarm spring into the girl's large black eyes. "I will not harm you," he said. "Hold still for just a minute and I'll get us loose and separated."

In an apologetic voice, he continued, "You were in the water and freezing. I knew of only one way to warm you quickly and perhaps even to save your life."

Ging remained tense and watchful. The man's use of her language was crude and heavily accented, still she understood him. She felt the pain from the splinters in her flesh, but for now that was a minor concern.

The blankets came free and Tom rolled away from the girl. He grabbed up his clothing from the ground and climbed erect. Hastily he began to draw on the damp shirt and trousers.

Ging looked at the leanly sinewed, young white man. He was tall and his legs seemed quite long, out of proportion as compared with the men of her race. Rope-like muscles rippled beneath his pale skin. He must be very strong.

She thought of her own nakedness. Her clothing was lost somewhere in the great depths of the sea. She stood up and started to pull the blanket around herself.

At her movement, a multitude of stabbing pains from her wounds came to sharp focus.

Tom saw Ging wince at the soreness of her

injuries. He spoke to her. "I can remove some of those splinters. Do you want me to try? Then we will go to San Francisco and find a doctor to take out the worst ones and put medicine on the hurts."

"Yes. Please do try." Slowly she unwrapped the covering and stood nude in front of him.

"Turn around so the sun will shine on you and then I can see better."

Tom pulled his jackknife from a pocket and knelt before the girl. Even on his knees, he was nearly as tall as she. He began to probe with the sharp point of the blade, removing one barb after another.

As he worked he spoke to her. "Why were you in the water?"

"The Keeper tried to kill me," she replied in a low whisper. "He hit me and threw me in the sea."

Tom had observed the purple bruises on her stomach and the side of her head. He cast a quick look into her face. It was icy with hate. He would ask no more questions. She would tell her story when she was ready.

"Do you have friends in San Francisco?" asked Tom.

"No. I know no one in America."

At one point, Tom had to dig deeply into her flesh to take out a fragment of wood. Ging quivered at the punch of the knife. Her full lips compressed to mere lines. She stared hard at the waves pounding the rocky beach and made no outcry. And she would not, regardless of the depth the blade was driven or the level of the pain.

Tom extracted the splinter and halted. Blood leaked in small rivulets from several of the injuries where he had probed most deeply, and clear, liquid beads of lymph had formed at the less severe punctures. The pain must be agonizing. Her face was strained and a rapid pulse beat visibly in her throat like a tiny trapped animal.

Ging's eyes shifted to Tom's suddenly, questioning. "Something is wrong that you stop?" she asked.

"I am sorry that I hurt you, but I cannot help it. Some of those slivers are driven quite far in. Yet I must get most of them out so your travel to San Francisco will be easier to bear."

"Please continue. The pain you make is not important." To feel pain means I am still alive when I could be dead, thought Ging. "You have saved my life and now you tend my wounds. I am very grateful."

Tom nodded. Her voice was husky with emotion. He began again.

He tried to ignore her nakedness and the smooth soft skin beneath his fingers. The mounds of her breasts contained several of the sharp wooden fragments and he was very conscious of her as he worked to withdraw the wooden shafts.

Ging ranged her sight out over the sea. She had survived after her enemy had done his best to kill her. He may try again. She would acquire a sharp knife and never again would she go unarmed.

She glanced at the face of the white man. His countenance was full of concern for her and concentration upon his task. He would make a fine friend. From this time onward, his foes would be hers. Her debt to him would be paid.

"That is all of the splinters I should try to take out," said Tom. "Let's now go to San Francisco and have a doctor complete the job. He will have better tools and perhaps something to deaden the pain."

He whistled the black horse to him and saddled it. He mounted. "Put the blanket around you in a way so that you can ride," Tom told Ging.

She did as directed. "I will need a belt or string to hold it in place," she said.

"Use this." Tom slid his belt from the loops of his trousers.

She buckled the leather strap about her waist to fasten the covering snugly. "I am ready. How do I get up?"

Tom moved backward to a spot behind the saddle. He leaned down and easily lifted her into the vacated seat.

The horse went at a gentle lope up the sloping flank of Mount Sutro and down the eastern side to San Francisco.

The black horse carried Ging and Tom along the streets of the city. People stopped to stare at the Chinese girl bundled in the blanket and the young white man. Tom paid them no attention and guided the mount directly to his lodging. He took her inside.

"You are welcome to stay here. I will send a doctor to treat you. Then I must go help some of your countrymen move from the docks to a barracks where they will be outfitted for the goldfields. I would like for you to stay here until I return. Will you do that?"

"I have no place to go. Thank you for your kindness."

"There is no food here, but I will bring some when I return."

"I will be waiting. My name is Ging Ti."

"I am Tom Gallatin. We will talk when I get back."

"Will you loan me your knife?" asked Ging.

Tom studied the girl. "You think this man, The Keeper, may be here in San Francisco?"

"I am certain he is. He may have seen me on the street and know I am alive."

Tom dug his knife from his pocket and handed it to Ging. "I certainly hope you were not recognized by anyone that would harm you. I should be back in two or three hours. There is an extra set of my clothes on the bed. They will be much too large for you, but you may wear them until we can buy some proper woman's clothing."

"I have no money for clothing," said Ging.

"I have enough," said Tom. Still he lingered and did not go. Should he leave her unprotected?

Ging saw the questioning expression on Tom's countenance. "I will be safe with this," she said and opened the blade of the jackknife.

"All right, then," Tom said. He left.

Tom left his horse at the livery and then stopped briefly at the physician's office and arranged for the man to make a call on Ging within the hour. Then he hurried to Yang's warehouse on the docks.

Tan Ke was impatiently pacing at the huge door of the building. When he saw Tom, he hastened to meet him.

"Where have you been?" Ke asked in an aggravated voice. "We have been waiting hours, since before daylight. Now the streets are crowded and we will have much trouble marching the men to the dormitories."

"Something happened that I had to take care of," responded Tom. He noted the anger in Yang's lieutenant. "How many men are there?"

"One hundred and ninety-nine. I have kept them in the warehouse and out of sight so nothing can be organized against us."

"Good. Line them up five abreast and in two groups about fifteen feet apart. That will allow room for me to cross between them so I can go to whichever side of the street the trouble comes."

They swung the door of the warehouse open. Within the cavernous building, the group of Chinamen rose to their feet. With their long queues and foreheads shaved for a third of the space across the top of their heads, they appeared quite alien.

Ke barked orders at the men and gestured with his hand for emphasis. They moved hastily to do as he directed.

Most men had shoulder poles to transport their skimpy possessions. A few had backpacks, and some merely carried their belongings in bundles in their arms. They jostled each other as Ke ordered them to squeeze close together. He wanted their formation to be as narrow as possible when they went along the dangerous streets.

"Walk fast, but do not run," Tom told the Chinamen. "Now move out."

Ke led the way at the head of the column. Tom took station on the left side near the middle. The group of men went at a swift stride on The Embarcadero. Their eyes uneasily roved about for they sensed the wariness of Tom and Ke.

White men shouted at them from the docks. Some ruffians and unemployed laborers began to gather at the rear of the column and tag along.

A white man cried out in a shrill, angry voice. "Damn heathen Chinaboys will work for a dime a day. A white man can't make a living with them taking all the jobs."

"Send them all back to China," shouted another man. "Cut off their pigtails for a starter." He ran forward and grabbed the queue of one of the Chinamen in the last line. The Chinaman jerked free before the man could wield his knife.

Tom dropped back to the growing throng of hecklers. "These men are going to the goldfields," he called out. "They will not stay in San Francisco."

"How in hell do we know that?" growled a big, hulking man drawing close to Tom. "We've been told that before, but the number of Chinamen in the city grows larger each day. They must not be given jobs here that we need."

A man pushed forward. He thrust a finger at Tom. "I say Ben here is right. I say you are a liar just like all the other guards that are hired to help these moon-eyed Celestials come off the ships. Maybe we should rough you up a little bit."

Tom stared back unblinkingly at the man. "Don't start something you can't finish. And I've told you the truth." He moved away. He had stopped the group temporarily as he had planned. He trotted to catch up with Ke and the drove of Chinamen.

Tom took position on the right side of the column. A square-built man in a blue uniform came out of the police station on the opposite side of the street and fell in to patrol that flank. He raised his hand in greeting.

Tom returned the salute of the policeman. Because of their dauntless courage, they were called Fearless Charlies by many of the townsfolk.

People on the street stopped to regard the procession. Some turned to follow.

A man left a saloon, noticed the crowd, and turned back through the door to call out. "Bunch of Chinamen coming up the street. Come outside and see what's happening. Should be a lot of fun."

Men streamed out to string along beside the moving assembly of Chinese. A dozen more men came from a card parlor. Other business places emptied a portion of the patrons. The throng swelled.

Strengthened by the growing numbers of supporters, the hecklers raised their angry shouts and curses to a roaring din. Though the Chinese did not comprehend the words, they recognized the dangerous intent and their eyes rolled with apprehension.

The ones on the outside pressed closer to the center of the column. One man dropped his shoulder pole and his belongings. The crush of men behind prevented him from retrieving it and all was trampled on the street.

A rough-looking man sprang out of the crowd and into the center of the avenue to bar the way. "You can't go any further," he bellowed. "Go back to China. We don't want you here."

Tom broke into a run to the front. If the procession was halted, the white hecklers would gain courage and very likely attack the Chinamen. Those men might panic and stampede in a wild scattering through the town. With the high emotion of the mob, many Chinese could be badly injured or killed.

The policeman, charging swiftly, reached the white man blocking the street before Tom could. The lawman barely slowed. He leaned forward and scooped the man up on his shoulder, lifted him bodily, and tossed him into the crowd at the edge of the street. He continued up to the fallen man, put his finger in the man's face, and told him something Tom could not hear.

The policeman spun around and scanned the rapidly enlarging horde of white men. He motioned for Ke to hurry on.

A half brick sailed from the swarm of white men. It struck a Chinaman in the head with a sodden crunch. The man fell to his knees. Two of his comrades grabbed him by the arms and carried him onward with them.

The policeman sprang into the horde of badgering men and dragged one out. He shoved the man, to send him sprawling.

"Get up and march straight back to the jailhouse," commanded the policeman.

"Finnegan, it's me, Casey," said the man as he scrambled to his feet. "Don't you know me?"

"I know you, Casey. Now get your ass back to my jail and wait there for me."

"Are you going to arrest me for hitting a Chinaman?" cried Casey.

"No. Not for that, but for causing me trouble on the streets. Now march before I lock you up for a year instead of a day."

"Damn you, Finnegan," cursed Casey. He swung about and stalked down the street.

The lawman came to walk beside Tom. "Better you let me handle the troublemakers. If you take them on, that could start a riot. You're not too bright in taking the Chinamen through town this time of day."

Tom said nothing. The policeman was correct.

"Get up there and tell that lead Chinaman to speed it up," said Finnegan. "Two more blocks and we'll be in Chinatown, and I'll turn this mob back there."

Handfuls of mud rained upon the Chinamen. A rock arced up and fell among them. Finnegan dropped back to walk between the Chinese and a knot of sullen men. The missiles stopped.

Tom ranged his view over the four hundred or so angry men and spectators. He did not believe the one lawman could prevent that army from pursuing the foreigners all the way to the dormitories. What they might do there worried Tom.

Ke reached Bush Street, the beginning of Chinatown. Finnegan trotted ahead to cross the street and stand on the curb. He shouted out in a loud, clarion voice. "Nobody but the Chinamen past this point."

A few white men turned aside or halted. Most continued straight at the policeman. He pulled his billy club from his belt for the first time.

gain, we begin the recess with the on
around," said one of the policemen.
"I'd . . . I'm glad to see you," Finnegan

Chapter 6

Finnegan caught the eye of the lead trouble-maker. He held his club up for all to see and motioned the man back.

"To hell with you," cursed the enraged man. "I'm going to follow these Chinaboys to their rat hole and burn them out."

"Not in my town." Finnegan's voice was a warning growl. He leaped forward and clouted the man on the head with his club.

The fellow fell hard on the street. Finnegan jumped back to the curb. He raised his club again and shouted, "No white man past here today!"

The lead rank of the troop of Chinamen has-tened past the policeman. He motioned impa-tiently for them to hurry.

Tom elbowed men from his way to go to stand by the wall of the corner building near Finnegan. The man looked at him and shook his head, telling Tom not to interfere.

Two uniformed policemen raced in from Kear-ney Street. They plowed a path to Finnegan.

"Captain. We heard the ruckus and came on the run," said one of the policemen.

"Good. Damn glad to see you. Thompson, go over to Pine Street and keep all white men from going in to Chinatown that way."

"Right, Captain." Thompson trotted off.

"O'Sullivan, take the other side of the street. Let no one past except Chinamen."

The man sprinted across Bush. He drew his billy club and started to smack it in the palm of his hand as he eyed the riled and milling throng.

The mob of white men peeled away from the string of Chinamen and dammed like a tide in front of the two policemen. But they did not disperse. Their wrathful cries and threats echoed on the walls of the tall building like low thunder.

The last of the Chinamen scurried by the policemen and plunged into Chinatown.

"It's all over, folks," called Finnegan. "All over. Now go on home."

"You bastard," screamed a maddened man. "You protected those heathen Chinaboys. Tomorrow they'll be on the docks or at one of the factories taking our jobs. I'll go to the city commissioners and they'll take your badge."

Finnegan laughed good-naturedly. "It's tough times when there's not enough jobs to go around. But I don't believe many men would want my job. Now go on back downtown and let this thing cool."

The roar of the throng gradually subsided. The men slowly disbanded, drifting down the hill toward the bay or off on one of the side streets.

Finnegan came to stand by Tom. "That was a near thing," the policeman said.

"I'd say you earned your pay today," Tom said.

"I need more officers," said Finnegan. He leaned against the building beside Tom and calmly rolled a cigarette. "I have sixty-two men to enforce the law in a city of one hundred and sixty thousand people. There are dozens of small private armies here, the tong societies and their soldiers, the brothel owners and enforcers, the saloon keepers' association, the bank protective association and others. Each one is trying to protect their property and profit. Most of them will kill to do that."

Finnegan stared coldly at Tom. "Are you listening? I might just tell you something of interest."

"I'm listening," replied Tom. He had much respect for the man after having watched him in action to control the mob. He had surely upheld the name Fearless Charlie.

"San Francisco has nearly six hundred places where you can buy whiskey. The city has the largest area of whorehouses of any town in the world. There are at least a thousand whores. Every race and nationality of men on earth is represented here. They gamble, fornicate, and fight and kill. I bet the honest man is a mighty small minority."

He gazed at Tom, though his thoughts seemed to be directed inward. Finally he spoke again. "Right now all I can do is keep the fights between the different factions in the alleys and out of the streets. The city could explode at anytime and there would be no safety anyplace.

Complete anarchy would easily overrun San Francisco."

Finnegan peered intently at Tom. "I would guess there are four hundred men killed each year in this town. Most of the bodies are never found, either dumped in the bay or buried. Also, dueling is a commonplace thing. There's about one a week. Maybe half end in a killing.

"Yesterday morning there was a duel on the east end of Angel Island. A ship's captain named Douchane was killed by a young man with a pistol. Now the island is out of my jurisdiction so I'll not try to do anything about the killing. I hear the duel was over some story that forty-three Chinamen died of food poisoning or ship fever at sea on the *Sierra Wind*. Well, I have a brother aboard that ship. Those tales of deaths were a lie. Douchane probably deserved to die, but not for the reason the duel was fought."

"You seem to be well informed," Tom said, his heart sinking at the news given so positively.

"I'm going to hold this town together. Therefore, I make it my business to know what is happening. You work for Mingren Yang. He is a shrewd heathen. He has joined as one of the head officers of the Chee Kong Tong, the most secret and violent in San Francisco. They are into a dozen rackets, from opium and slave girl smuggling to murder. I recommend you quit him at once and get a decent job."

"Like what?"

"I could use an honest law officer. The pay is five dollars a day."

"I make twice that."

"Why do you? Think about that. Come by the station and talk with me sometime. Meanwhile trust no one." Finnegan walked off down Bush Street.

Mulling over what the police captain had told him, Tom went west to Stockton Street and turned right. He entered the side door of a large, two-story barracks.

Ke was collecting money from the newly arrived Chinamen. Two other of Yang's employees were passing out rolls of matting, mining tools and provisions to the would-be gold miners.

"Do you need any help?" Tom asked Ke.

"No," replied Ke in a surly voice. "Tell Honorable Yang these men will be ready to cross the bay on the ferry in the morning. Do not be late again."

Tom did not respond. He noted the big bruises on Ke's cheek where a stone had hit him.

Tom left the building and retraced his steps one block to Dupont Street and went left to Yang's establishment. The Chinaman sat silently as Tom entered the office just off the bookkeeping section.

"You were two hours late to help Ke this morning," said Yang.

Tom nodded briefly. He kept his expression noncommittal.

"That caused much trouble and interference of the policemen. I do not like what has happened." Yang stared into the flinty eyes of the young white man.

There will be no apology, thought Tom. "You

have been informed correctly as to the events," said Tom.

"You spent the night on the beach of the ocean and then this morning returned with a beautiful Chinese woman. What bait did you use to catch such a prize?"

"Only simple luck," replied Tom. He sensed Yang did not want a complete break with him.

"If she is as beautiful as I have heard, she is worth much gold. A physician came to visit her. Is she badly hurt?"

"No," Tom said. The man must have many spies on the street.

"She must belong to someone. How else could a Chinese girl come to San Francisco? The rightful owner could come at any time to claim her."

"One person cannot own another," said Tom. He remembered Chun Zheng's statement that Yang owned her.

Yang's lips spread in a whimsical smile. "You may be incorrect in that assumption."

"Ke said the men that arrived today will be outfitted and ready to cross the bay on the ferry tomorrow morning," Tom said, wanting to change the subject.

"Very good. Guide them to the docks before daylight. I will arrange for the ferry to make an early morning run. Go across the bay with them and be certain they are given directions for the right road to take.

"There is something else I wish for you to do for me. Seventy-nine Chinese virgins arrived on the schooner *Cloud Racer* this morning. There will be an auction of thirty of them at 410 Beale Street beginning this evening at nine P.M. Go there and identify as many of the bidders as possible. We must especially know who is behind the sale, who brought the girls into this country. Try to find that out. Ask questions."

"Why are you interested in slave girls?" Tom questioned. He had a feeling that Yang already knew part of the answers.

"This traffic in my countrywomen must cease. I must have information to stop it."

"How do I get in? Won't they have guards?"

"Most certainly they will have guards. A friend of mine works in the building. Look for him in one of the windows. Do as he says. Once you are inside, act like you have been invited and are one of the spectators. Wear your pistol, for you may have need for it."

Yang's eyes bore into Tom. "Why did you move out of your residence here? Was it not pleasant?"

"I'm used to more freedom and distance from people," answered Tom. He arose. "I will see to those things you have mentioned." In an elemental way, Tom knew the Chinaman meant him no good. But why?

"It was delectable," said Ging, daintily wiping her fingers and smiling her thanks at Tom. "I was practically raised on fish as food. On the voyage from Canton we never had fish once, and that with the ocean full of them all about. They gave us only salt pork, dried beef, hard biscuits and beans. And now and then a lime."

"You are welcome to the food. I was starving, too." On his return Tom had stopped at a restaurant on Sutter near his lodging and purchased a jug of hot tea and three dishes of Chinese food. They had eaten and talked.

She was dressed in his shirt and trousers, with the cuffs of both garments turned up in a large roll. Her black, almond eyes shone at him, luminous as lanterns.

Tom had never felt so good in the presence of another person, man or woman. He relaxed, allowing himself the keen enjoyment of listening to her musical, lilting voice and watching her feminine movements. Did he feel this way because he had pulled her from the ocean almost dead? Did he think in some manner she belonged to him? He recalled what Yang had said about owning another human.

"My wounds have been treated and I am wonderfully full of excellent food. I owe all this to you," said Ging.

"Tell me how you came to be in the sea," said Tom.

Ging's happy visage faded and took on a hunted, haunted look. "Zaishing Mo tried to kill me."

"He is the one you referred to before as The Keeper?"

"Yes. The Keeper. He was the man who came to Canton and purchased eighty women for a merchant here in San Francisco. I was one of those he bought."

"You were agreeable to being bought?"

Ging told Tom of the storm and the destruction of the family's fishing junk. She explained how she and her father had sold her for four hundred dollars in gold. And she told of the happenings on the long voyage across the ocean.

"Can we still be friends?" asked Ging, her eyes sad and misty.

"I would like very much to be your friend. What was the merchant's name who bought the women?"

"The Keeper never told us."

"I shall be watching for this Zaishing Mo. There is to be an auction of thirty girls tonight. From what you have said, they must be part of the very ones you crossed the ocean with."

"Do not tell them or any other person about me," said Ging. "Everyone must continue to believe I am dead. In that way, I shall be safe."

"I will say nothing. But enough of those times. Tell me about the South China Sea. I have heard tales of it from seamen on the docks. I would like to hear of it from someone who lived there."

"One thing I am certain of, the water is much warmer there," laughed Ging. She recalled the memories of her childhood and described them to Tom.

"I would like to go there one day and sail with your father," said Tom. "I have been thinking of going to sea since I came here."

Tom climbed to his feet. "Now to buy you something to wear other than my pants and shirt. Stand up and let me measure you against my body so I'll know what size dress to buy."

Ging rose and put her head on Tom's chest. "Stand like this?" she asked.

"Yes. You are about this tall," Tom said and brought his hand from the top of her head to touch a button on his shirt. He estimated her weight. "What colors do you like?"

"All colors," smiled Ging.

"I will return soon. I have never purchased clothing or anything for a girl."

"I will like whatever you buy," promised Ging.

Tom slept in the afternoon. When he awoke, darkness was settling into the room. Ging was near the window and peeking out through the curtains.

He had bought her two dresses, a pair of shoes and a coat. One dress was blue and the other yellow. She now wore the blue one. That had been Tom's favorite also.

Ging heard him stir and turned to speak. "There is one of my countrymen in the street and he often looks in this direction. He is dressed in old clothes and sits in that doorway partway up the block. I believe he is watching this house."

Tom came to stand beside her. Fog was collecting in the street and drifting up the slope of the hill in wispy clouds. The raggedly dressed man sat smoking a cigarette.

"I do not recognize him," Tom said.

"A man who spies on us cannot be a friend," Ging said. "Do you think it is a person looking for me?"

"The man probably has nothing to do with either of us," said Tom. "I must now go to Beale Street and watch the auction. I do not know how long these things require, but if they sell all thirty of the girls tonight, it may take considerable time to complete the bidding. Describe this Zaishing Mo for me so I will know him if I see him."

"He is very flat-faced," said Ging. "He is quite broad and very strong. Believe nothing he should say and be on your guard against tricks," she concluded.

"Keep the door locked," cautioned Tom. He buckled on his gun, and slid into his coat and hat and went out the door.

The mist had thickened on the street. Tom struck out along Mason. It was only a ten-minute walk to Beale. Ahead of him, a lamplighter moved from one streetlight to the next, reaching up with his flaming torch to touch off the wicks.

Chapter 7

Whittiker finished his food and glanced at his watch. "It is one o'clock," he said to Coldiron. "There will be men upstairs waiting to take your gold."

The two men were eating in the sumptuous dining room of the Grand Hotel in the Harpenning Block of Market Street. The polite waiters in their formal uniforms had served them with elegant aplomb. The main course of fresh ocean fish was especially pleasing to Luke, a delightful change from the red meat available in the inland country.

"I'm ready," said Luke. He smiled at his friend. To gamble with unknown men for high stakes, a contest of skill and a duel of wits and nerve, was a risky and yet an enjoyable passion. At the end of this action, someone would walk away winner of one hundred and twenty-five thousand dollars. That was a fortune when a good meal could be purchased for fifty cents or less. But not in the Grand Hotel.

They left the dining room, crossed the thick wool carpet of the foyer, and climbed the three flights of stairs to the fourth floor of the hotel. They continued to a private banquet room at the front. One round table covered with green felt was in the center of the room. An unlit chandelier hung over the table.

Five men were grouped and talking near one of the big windows overlooking the street. The hotel manager and a waiter stood at a distance, quietly waiting. All turned as Whittiker and Coldiron entered the room.

"There's one fellow here I don't know," Sam said to Luke as they crossed the room.

"Hello," Sam called out to the men. "I would like to introduce my friend, Luke Coldiron, from Colorado. Luke, this first man is Jeremiah Trenton."

Trenton put out his hand. He was a slender man of middle age. He smiled broadly and had a pleasant, sonorous voice.

Dan Tarter was a giant of a man with massive, powerful hands. Luke exerted his own strong grip to keep his fingers from being mangled.

Albert McCubbin, stiff and somber, shook hands without a word.

André Beaulieu was a hatchet-faced man. The scars of smallpox made him look as if a gun had exploded and torn gaping wounds in his cheeks and chin.

Whittiker ceased his introductions and looked quizzically at the unknown man.

"I am Randall Fallon," said the man. "I happened to be in town on business and heard of this game. I would like to play with you. I have sufficient money." He touched the front of his jacket with a finger.

Luke studied Fallon. He was above average height and quite fair-skinned with blond hair. His movements were smooth and precise. Though he smiled, his gray eyes were flat and had a penetrating, probing quality. A fearless man, Luke judged.

"Does anyone here know Mr. Fallon?" asked Whittiker.

"I am not acquainted with any of these men," said Fallon. "But Mr. Stevenson of the bank just down the street knows me. I have been discussing with him the purchase of a clipper ship."

"Where are you from?" queried Whittiker.

"From New Orleans, Louisiana, if my home is important to know." There was an edge in Fallon's tone. "Gentlemen, if you do not want me to play, merely tell me and I shall leave."

Tarter laughed in a deep bass voice. "Hell. I'm going to watch all of you fellows to see that the game stays friendly, so I might as well watch one more man. I say let him sit in. What do you think, Coldiron?"

Luke shrugged. "It makes no difference to me one way or the other."

"Then let's play poker," said Tarter.

As the men seated themselves around the table, the hotel manager approached. "Thank you gentlemen for selecting the Grand Hotel for your game. This young man is Andy. He will bring whatever you need, fresh cards, food and drink, or deliver a message. He will be at your service as long as the playing continues. When you break for rest, merely tell him when to return."

"Thank you, Mr. Florintin," said Whittiker. "You have arranged things perfectly. The men are ready to buy chips, so please bring the cards and guards."

"At once," said Florintin.

"While he is doing that, let us agree on the rules of play," Whittiker said to all the players. "At this late date, I would say Mr. Fallon should not attempt to change the rules already decided. The game is five-card draw poker. There are no wild cards, no limits to size of bets or number of raises. Money will be all cash, gold or paper. Twenty-five thousand dollars is the original and only purchase of chips. When that is lost, you are out of the game. You may stay and observe if you wish. There will be no other spectators allowed except Mr. Florintin and me. A white chip will be worth one hundred dollars, blue five hundred and red one thousand.

"You are all businessmen, therefore you may have visitors. You will talk with them outside in the hall so as not to bother the other players.

"The periods of play shall be sixteen hours followed by eight hours of rest, until the number of players is reduced to two. At that point, they can decide how they want to continue the game. This room, the food and beverages cost one hundred dollars a day. It is to be paid for by the winner. Are there any objections to any portion of these conditions?"

The men spoke their agreement as Florintin and two men with shotguns came into the room. Florintin carried a steel box to the table and set it down. He unlocked it and removed a rack of chips and several sealed decks of cards.

"Gentlemen, your money please. I shall exchange it for chips. Then all the money will be locked in this box and Mr. Whittiker and I and these guards will take it to the bank vault. At the end of play, the winner shall go and claim the currency. Mr. Whittiker and I shall again be present at that transaction."

The men brought gold and paper money from their pockets and piled it on the table. The gold coins glittered like yellow jewels among the dingy greenbacks.

Florintin carefully counted the currency and replaced it with the brightly colored chips. He locked the money in the steel box.

"The key shall be left with the safe in the vault of the bank. I believe the winner will certainly receive his reward. Between periods of play you may leave your chips in the hotel safe."

Florintin picked up the box. Whittiker and the two guards fell in behind him and they filed from the room.

"Let's begin," said McCubbin.

The deal rotated from player to player. Beaulieu was on Luke's left, then came Trenton, Fallon, McCubbin and Tarter.

Each time Luke had the deck, he felt for identifying marks that someone might have put on some of the cards. He did not expect to find any or to catch anyone manipulating the cards for a crooked deal. If that happened, it would occur much later when men became tired, less observant and alert.

At the end of four hours, Coldiron had won five thousand dollars. He had played conservatively, studying the style and mannerisms of his adversaries.

Near the end of the seventh hour, Luke sensed the pattern of the game shift. Some method to control the fall of the cards had come into force.

He gave no sign of his suspicions. He played cautiously and his hooded eyes scrutinized the actions of every player. The sharper would periodically alter his tactics, but he could not avoid Luke's detection for long.

Besides Coldiron, Fallon and Tarter were winners. The blond man had retained his twenty-five thousand dollars and added to that mound of his chips another fifteen thousand or so. Tarter was ahead about two thousand dollars.

Luke concentrated on Fallon, watching the man's supple hands move with swift, oiled flow, deft and effortlessly. Luke remembered the fellow's handshake. There had been calluses at places on the palm and thumb from much practice with a pistol. Luke had seen his kind before, a professional gambler, and gunman when the need arose. However, Luke could not discover Fallon cheating.

Beaulieu's scarred face was pinched and had begun to turn a deeper red as he lost. His shuffle and deal appeared honest.

Trenton had played a lax game and was the biggest loser. He was now chewing his lower lip and it looked ready to bleed. His deal was straight.

McCubbin was a thick-boned man with a large stomach. His hands were clumsy. Sometimes he dropped the deck as he shuffled, or would skid the cards inaccurately across the playing board to the other men when he dealt. At first he laughed good-naturedly at these times. Now he was morose and silent.

The giant Tarter raked the cards to him and took them into his mammoth hands. The deck disappeared under those broad palms and thick, blunt-ended fingers.

As Luke watched, Tarter began to shuffle. In the middle of the process, one of Tarter's knuckles bent when it should not have. He had positioned a card in the deck for later retrieval as he desired.

Coldiron felt his heart pound a few beats. He had found the trickster. Tarter was the sharper and dealing winning hands to his partner, Fallon. Tarter's awkward-looking hands misled the eye. They were in truth amazingly proficient at crooked dealing.

The remainder of the scheme unfolded before Coldiron as the game continued. Tarter controlled the cards one time out of six hands played. In the other five, the cards fell at random as they should. Both Fallon and Tarter played those deals skillfully and won more than their share. They bet against each other if the remaining players dropped out early in the hand.

Fallon stood ready to carry out the final conclusion of the scheme. Any player complaining of the honesty of the game would challenge Fallon, for he was the obvious big winner. The gunman would demand an apology. If none was forthcoming and the accuser failed to back down, Fallon would fight the battle. Tarter would be safe.

The two sharpers would soon drive all the players from the game. Luke had no intention of letting it come to that end. He made his own plans. First there would be more cheating—then the battle. The bet that took the one hundred and fifty thousand dollars would not be on the cards, but on who lived through the killing time.

The three honest men were going to be robbed of every dollar. Luke mulled that for a moment. Then he shoved the concern aside. They had to lose so that the last deadly hand could be played.

Coldiron gave himself winning cards every time he dealt. Though he shifted techniques often, he knew someone would eventually find him out. Fallon would be the most likely man to spot the crooked maneuver.

Andy announced the hotel chef had made fresh sandwiches. Did anyone want to eat?

The players called a break and paced the room to unwind from the tension. Andy brought food and wine. The men ate standing up.

Luke took his food and drink and watched out the window into the night. A dense fog with a light drizzle had moved in. The street lamps were islands of light in the mist. From his observation point on the fourth floor, the night strollers, muffled in coats, were mere blobs of black moving in the fog-dimmed glare of the gaslights.

The game recommenced. During the next few hours, Luke added fifteen thousand dollars to his winnings. He won a substantial portion of the sum during the hands dealt by the honest players, for then he bet aggressively, knowing the cards fell randomly and skill would win. Trenton's luck was the worst Luke had ever witnessed. The man contributed significantly to Luke's growing horde of chips.

Fallon caught on to Coldiron's double-dealing game. He began to cheat, giving strong hands to Tarter. It was Coldiron against the two of them.

An hour later, Trenton flipped his last chip onto the green felt of the playing table. "That's for the winner of the next hand," he said. "I assume that will be one of you three." His eyes were full of malice as he ranged them over Fallon, Tarter and Coldiron. He had been caught in a battle of crooked cards and knew it. Without a word, he left the room.

The night grew old as the game continued. Luke was maintaining his pile of chips, but only by taking them from McCubbin and Beaulieu.

McCubbin had begun to frequently check his watch. With audible relief in his voice, he announced, "It has been sixteen hours. Time for a break and some rest." He raked his small quantity of chips into his hand and stood up.

"It is five in the morning," said Tarter. "Shall we meet back here at one, just after lunch, and begin again?"

The men silently nodded. They moved toward the doorway that led down to the lobby.

Without comment the players placed their chips in large envelopes that Florintin gave them, sealed the flaps, and signed their names across the seal. Florintin locked all away in the hotel safe.

"Your possessions shall be undisturbed until you return," the hotelman promised.

Coldiron followed the other players out onto the street and watched them separate and go off in different directions. Because of the cheating, he had hoped the game would end tonight.

He pulled his coat collar up around his neck and stepped from under the awning of the hotel entrance. He lifted his head and breathed deeply, smelling the damp brick and the more pungent odor of horse manure on the street.

He could see stars here and there. The sky was clearing. He walked toward Whittiker's home.

Chapter 8

In the fog and drizzle Tom circled the three-story building on Beale Street. It appeared to be some kind of factory. He observed not one sign of human activity or crack of light in the window on any floor.

As he started his second turn, he saw a man midway the length of the structure descend a flight of steps from the street level and not reemerge. He looked down into the stairwell as he passed. It was empty.

Tom continued on, turning the corner, and found a window open that had not been before. He slowed to peer at it.

"Are you Yang's man?" a Chinese man's voice asked from the blackness of the window.

"Yes."

"Then climb inside. Hurry before you are seen."

Tom muscled himself through and into the pitch black of the building. He pulled his six-gun and strained to see the man and the surroundings.

"This way. Take hold of me and I will guide you," said the man.

Tom clasped the man's small, bony shoulder. He sensed they were passing through room after room and along hallways. It would not be easy to find his way out alone.

Finally they stopped. There was the scrape of boards as a trapdoor was lifted aside.

"Go down," said the voice.

"And then what?" Tom could barely make out the deeper gloom of the hole.

"When your eyes are more accustomed to the dark, you will see a light ahead. That light is where the sale will be held. Go there. Just before it is over, come back here and I will lead you out."

"Who knows of this way of getting inside?"

"Only I know. I have worked here many years. I found it by accident and have kept it secret on Honorable Ing's orders. Now Yang has asked me to use it for his purpose. Even the present owners of the building do not know of its existence."

Tom felt for the steps and went down into the darkness. He held his gun ready and waited for his eyes to adjust to the small quantity of light. He put a hand out and felt a stone wall. He judged it would be part of the interior support of the tall building.

Gradually a section of the gloom that surrounded him began to lighten. He walked in that direction, moving cautiously through the sour dampness of the subterranean depths of the building. He heard voices, distorted by the tunnel-like corridor. They grew louder as he proceeded.

He reached a cross tunnel of stone. To the

left, fifty feet or so distant, a man in seaman's garb and armed with a shotgun stood at a door. Tom guessed that would be the entrance the man on the street had used.

To the right was a well-lighted room of a large size. The floor was of wood and the walls were paneled with the same material. Four chandeliers with several gaslights on each brightly illuminated the space.

A low stage affair took up one end of the room. A black curtain was drawn, hiding whatever might be on the stage. Two dozen or so chairs, arranged in a double row, were positioned to view the stage. All but two of the seats were occupied, by men.

Tom entered and took a chair beside a middle-aged man. Tom looked straight ahead. He did not want any conversation.

Two Chinamen came into the room. Tom caught their movement from the corner of his eye and twisted to look. At that instant, one of the men swung his sight over the crowd. His eyes locked with Tom's.

The man had a flat face, appearing almost concave. And he was strongly built. Tom felt his heart hammer on his ribs. The man could be Zaishing Mo, The Keeper that Ging had described.

The man's eyes slipped away. He and the second man crossed the room, stepped up on the stage, and went behind the curtain.

The fellow fit the characteristics of The Keeper and he acted as if he were part of the operation to sell the slave girls. The very same girls Ging had crossed the ocean with. He had to be the same man.

Tom rotated his chair so he could easily see anybody leaving the room. As long as he knew Mo was here, Ging should be safe.

"Is this your first sale?" asked the man near Tom.

"Yes," said Tom.

"Are you going to buy a girl?"

"No."

"Just as well since there is a law against the sale of slave girls. It is not enforced strictly now, but one day it will be. The men who buy and use the girls could be in much trouble."

"Then why are the sales held?"

"Though we sit here and watch, we could never testify we saw a sale," said the man. "We have simply seen a stage play. A cunning scheme, don't you think? The seller and buyer exchange money and merchandise in private."

"Who is the seller of these girls?"

"Nobody knows except the auctioneer. He will never tell."

The black curtains swept back. A young Chinese girl, her head lowered, stood on a raised dais in the center of the stage. The auctioneer, a white man, stood at the girl's side.

He spoke to the seated men below the stage. "You all know the rules, but I will repeat them. There must be no noise or signals except from those men bidding. The initial bid must be at least one thousand dollars. Each bid thereafter must be one hundred dollars or better. Now look closely at this lovely girl. She is fifteen years old. She is a virgin. I have a doctor's statement to that effect. Who will begin the bidding at one thousand?"

The auctioneer reached out and raised the chin of the girl. The light played upon the curves and planes of her beautiful face, and on her hair, black as a slice of midnight. She was clothed in a white silk gown that clung to the womanly contours of her body.

Tom felt sadness for the girl. He saw the mixture of fright and uncertainty on her face, and yet there was a resoluteness there to go through with the auction. She was on the stage of reality, where the harshness of life was being acted out.

Was she like Ging? wondered Tom. Had she deliberately sold herself to help her family? Was he seeing the strength and sacrifice of one girl for her family? Or had she been taken by force or trickery and transported to this faraway land with all the rewards going to her abductors?

"Do I have a bid for a thousand dollars?" asked the auctioneer.

A hand appeared.

"I have a bid. Do I have one for eleven hundred?"

"Fifteen hundred," said a second man.

A third man spoke. "Two thousand."

The bidding continued swiftly. The girl sold for thirty-three hundred dollars. The purchaser climbed upon the stage and went out through a door on the side of the stage with the auctioneer and the girl.

Tom looked around for The Keeper. He was not in sight.

Tom spoke quickly to the man seated beside him. "Does that side door lead to the outside?"

"Not directly, but there is a passageway that winds around to the door that we entered by."

Tom leaped up and ran from the room. He dashed along the corridor toward the seaman and the outside door. There was no time to retrace his path up and out through the labyrinth of the first floor.

The guard saw Tom coming and moved to block his way. He clutched his shotgun more firmly and raised it partway.

"Let me out," cried Tom. "A friend of mine needs help."

"No customer leaves once the bidding starts. Those are my orders from the boss." The man looked more closely at Tom. "How did you get in here? Not through this door."

Tom ignored the question. "Didn't you let two men out a short while ago?"

"Yes, but they are part of the sale operation."

Tom's hand plunged down for his six-gun. He brought it up. At the same time, he sprang forward and grabbed the barrel of the shotgun and held it from swinging to point at him. He jabbed the pistol in the guard's stomach.

"Now step out of the way. I don't want to kill you, but I'm leaving. Put your gun on the floor. Quickly.

"Now back up over there," ordered Tom. The seaman hastily bent to lay his shotgun down. Tom wrenched the door wide and leaped outside. He sprinted up the grade of the mist-filled street.

He dodged a horse and carriage, and raced on. No one else was on the street.

Mason Street formed out of the fog. Tom turned along it and slowed to a swift, silent stride. A light shone in the window of his apartment. He crept to the glass pane and looked inside through a gap in the curtains.

Ging was clamped within the arms of the Chinaman who had been with Mo in the building on Beale Street. The man was staring down at The Keeper lying on the floor.

The Keeper's face was twisted in pain. He held his stomach with both hands. Blood spurted between his fingers.

His chest heaved and shuddered as he tried to breathe. Then he grew very still.

Tom jumped to the entrance of the apartment. The lock had been broken. He flung it open. In one long stride he was inside and charging at Ging's captor. He had to reach the man before he could draw a weapon.

The Chinaman flung the girl aside and charged strongly forward to meet Tom. They crashed together.

Tom smashed the man savagely in the face with his fists. The shorter man rolled with the blows and grabbed Tom by the coat front. He hurled himself backward, pulling Tom to the floor with him. As they thudded down, he kicked Tom viciously in the stomach. Tom lost his wind with a swish. He hit the man and broke free. He surged to his feet.

The man was equally quick, vaulting erect. His hands dove inside his blouse and came out with a two-edged dagger. He jumped toward Tom.

Tom yanked his six-gun. He did not want to shoot the man here and make a loud noise. He hurled himself from in front of him. As he faded away, he extended his arm full length and swung the pistol mightily against the man's head. The vibration of the iron weapon shattering bone ran up Tom's arm.

The Chinaman's rush veered aside, his eyes unseeing. He slammed into the wall and crumpled against it.

Tom hurried to kneel beside Ging. "Are you hurt?"

"No. Only shaken up."

Tom blew out the light and listened for someone to come and inquire about the noise. A minute passed and then another. All remained quiet.

He cracked the door and peered outside. The fog lay motionless. The streetlight in the next block was a dull yellow stain on the drizzly night.

"I must get rid of these dead men," Tom told Ging. "I'll go and put that light out and be right back."

He stepped outside and hurried along the street. Ging saw his shadow at the light, then all went dark. A moment later he returned.

"Be very quiet," Tom said to Ging. "I'm going to carry these bodies far away. We could be in great trouble if I am seen."

He left with The Keeper over his shoulder. As he plodded with his burden, the drizzle became a rain, large cold drops plummeting out of the foggy black sky and drumming on the ground. He was thankful for the rain. It would hide him in his grisly task.

He made a second trip with a body. As he returned, he relit the street lamp.

Ging straightened the room and cleaned the

blood of The Keeper from the floor. When Tom entered, she was standing pale and drawn in the center of the room.

She whispered to Tom. "I had to fight The Keeper, for he was going to kill me. I waited until he came very close, then I cut him with your knife." She held out her hands and they were shaking. She looked up at Tom, her eyes black pools of torment.

Tom tenderly touched her face. "You did what had to be done. Have no remorse for the death of such a mean man."

"Please hold me," she said, her voice thin as a ghost's.

He wrapped her in his arms and held her for a long time. Finally she extracted herself. "I am so very cold," she said and went to lie on the bed, and pulled the covers around her. Tom put out the light and reclined beside her.

Ging took hold of his arm. He was a tough and fearless man. She was glad he was near. She closed her eyes.

Tom felt Ging tremble as she relived the killing of Zaishing Mo. She moaned, a sobbing echo on the night. Tom's heart cramped at the sound.

He drew Ging to him as a hard, brittle burst of rain rattled on the glass pane of the window.

Chapter 9

Tom came out onto the street when the daylight was nothing but a fainter tone of black in the east. He set off immediately for Yang's dormitories on Stockton Street.

Ke had the Chinamen prepared to travel when Tom arrived. The men formed into a silent column. The remembrances of the mob and the violence of yesterday were still visible in their faces as they cast worried looks about the street.

"How many groups?" Tom asked Ke.

"Four. I believe they have good headmen."

Tom knew they would have divided themselves as much as possible, based upon their surnames. In this manner they would feel some degree of family relationship, though often far removed in the past.

"Do not talk loudly," Tom told them. "Stay together, for to get separated will give the bullyboys the chance to hurt you. Ke, let's go."

"Right," Ke said and trotted to a lead position and set a fast pace. The men hoisted their shoulder poles or packs and strung out behind him. They wore all their clothes, as many as three layers, one over the other. Only one article of clothing had been adopted from the Americans—heavy work boots had replaced their low-cut slippers.

A few white men were encountered on their way to early jobs. No words were spoken or threats given. The cold morning twilight was not the time for hot hate or violence.

The ferry had steam pressure built and was waiting. Tom and Ke took their charges straight on board. The captain called down from the wheelhouse and the two deckhands threw off the hawsers, releasing the ferry's hold on the pier.

Tom climbed the ladder and entered the wheelhouse. The captain turned quickly, and Tom could see in his face he was ready to tell a Chinaman to get out. The man's expression altered abruptly at sight of Tom.

"Chilly on the water," said Tom.

"Yep. Stand by the fire if you want," said the captain.

Tom moved to the potbellied iron stove and spread his hands.

"Any trouble coming across town?" asked the captain.

"None."

"That's good. There's going to be a real blowup between white men and the Celestials one of these days soon. Your job as guard for them is going to become downright risky."

Tom did not reply. He also believed the conflict was coming and Finnegan would not be able to prevent it. He knew the Chinamen would get the worst of it.

Tom went to the window beside the captain and glanced down at the forward deck. Part of the Chinamen were at the railing and staring to the east at the mainland. Against the orange glow of the morning sky, the curved shadowy spine of San Pablo Ridge looked like some great crouching animal. Tom wondered if the Chinamen saw something ominous in the form of the ridge, or were they in their mind's eye already scooping up precious golden nuggets from some mountain stream?

The ferry passed Treasure Island and drew near to the coast. Tom could make out Oakland, a town of six or seven thousand people that had grown up around the docks. The vessel slowed and coasted into its berth. The deck crew made fast.

"Wait for me and one Chinaman," Tom told the captain. "We want to go back to San Francisco with you."

"All right. I see a few early passengers. I'll load them. Yang shouldn't mind if I make a little extra profit on the return trip."

Tom and Ke led the gold seekers to the far side of Oakland. "This is the road shown on your map," Tom told the headmen and pointed ahead at a wagon road heading northeast.

"Have you practiced how to pronounce the names of the towns you will pass through on the way?"

"Yes."

"Good," Tom said. "From time to time, ask people where you are so that you will not become lost. However, you are heading for the mountains and soon you will be able to see them. Do not be tricked by liars who may try to direct you the wrong way."

"We will be watchful," one of the headmen said.

"You should not have trouble from white men in the country. The cities are the worst places for that."

"We understand," said a headman. "Soon we shall return with much gold. You will hear us singing as we come."

"I would like to hear that," Tom said. "Good luck to all of you."

The headmen walked to their groups. The men shouldered their mining tools and provisions and moved along the muddy road. Their step was light and they began to talk to each other. Tom heard a man laugh in high spirits. They were very brave men to have traveled halfway around the world to an alien land and now to march into unknown mountains full of danger.

Tom and Ke returned to San Francisco on the ferry. They disembarked and walked together to the landward end of the dock.

"Tell Yang I will have something to eat and then come and report to him," said Tom.

"I am sure he will want to know what happened at the sale of the virgins last night," Ke said.

"I'm certain he will," said Tom. He veered aside from Ke's course. He wanted to be alone to do some thinking about the situation he was becoming embroiled in as Yang's guard. He proceeded north on The Embarcadero for a ways before he turned up one of the hill streets.

He soon found himself in the Barbary Coast. Many saloons, card parlors and brothels crowded the avenues. The morning was still early and only a few patrons were entering the places of business.

Tom entered a block crowded with older buildings fronting the street on both sides. Numerous doorways and windows opened onto the sidewalk.

A low musical chant of the voices of women sounded from along the block. Though the litany was an announcement of bodies and sensual delight for sale, Tom thought he heard a mournful, unhappy core to it.

He recognized the place as the Street Of The Slave Girls, one of the most infamous crib areas and a place of the cheapest whores. Each woman had a window where she sat to display herself to the men on the street, and a little room in which to ply her trade. The Chinese men called the women Chinoise, daughters of joy, and the white men, singsong girls. It was the meanest of all places for the women. Their life expectancy was short, usually less than five years. Death came either from disease, or by their own hand.

Tom quickened his pace. His wanderings had taken him out of his way. He would go to his apartment and eat with Ging.

"Tom Gallatin," a woman called in a plaintive voice.

Tom stopped and pivoted around. A young woman looked at him through the narrow latticework that covered the window of one of the rooms. She was heavily rouged and wore a low-bodiced dress.

"I am Chun Zheng. Don't you remember me?" she asked, her black eyes accusing him. "I told you Mingren Yang would sell me for the cribs and you did not believe me. Well, see for yourself." She ended on a high, almost hysterical note.

Tom stepped closer, peering into the tiny room through the lattice. He was jolted by the girl being here.

"God, I'm sorry. I did not think he would do such a thing." Beneath the bright whore paint, there was pain and fear in Chun's face. Tom felt a sharp lance of guilt.

"You are a fool and your eyes are blind." Her voice ended in a sob.

"What can I do for you? Do you want to leave this place?"

"Oh! Yes!" Chun cried in a wistful, hopeful tone. "But my new owner would never allow me. There are protectors watching us at this very moment. They are fierce men who keep the drunks and the strange, cruel men from beating us. But they also force us to stay here."

"Your owner and the protectors be damned. No person can own another. I told Yang that. Come out of there and go with me."

"Yes! Oh, yes! I am coming. Do not leave without me." Her door opened and she hastened to Tom.

"Hey, you there, what's going on?" shouted a white man from a doorway on the opposite side of the street. "You can't take girls from the cribs."

Tom ignored the man. "Come on," he said to Chun. Taking her by the hand, he started along the street.

The man ran to intercept them. "Take her back," he ordered. He slowed and advanced upon Tom with knotted fists.

A second white man came from a doorway ahead of Tom. "Charlie, do you need some help?" he shouted.

"No, Ed. There's just one man that's causing trouble. I can handle him." Charlie bore in, reaching for Chun.

Tom caught the outstretched arm, vising it tightly with his hand. He slugged the man in the side of the face. Instantly Tom hit again and heard bones break in the man's jaw.

Charlie crumpled. The second white man gave a shrill, keening whistle.

Almost immediately, two Chinamen popped out of the doorways and threw fast looks about to locate the call for assistance. They saw Tom and the man on the street at his feet. They rushed toward him, their thick queues flying out behind.

"Now you are going to get the worst beating a man ever had," said the white man.

The pair of Chinamen halted beside the white man. The three protectors closed on Tom.

He pushed Chun out of the way against the wall. He would try to put the larger white man out of the fight first. He spun around to face his assailants.

The white man had attacked more swiftly than Tom had anticipated and was already within striking range. A big fist lashed out to wallop Tom in the mouth.

Tom felt the jarring pain. The taste of blood was suddenly copper and salt in his mouth. He stepped toward the man, taking a hard blow to the body as he pounded aside his defense. Then Tom was inside and he struck Ed fiercely with a left and right.

The man went to his knees. Tom kicked him savagely in the face, knocking him backward to the ground.

One of the Chinamen hit Tom a solid blow to the side of the face. At the same time, the second man pummeled him in his lower back over his spine.

Tom whirled toward the man on his left. The man twisted and sprang away, his long queue swung out. Tom caught the big braid of hair and yanked the Chinaman rearward. He clouted the man solidly in the back of the neck, slamming him face down on the street.

The last man jumped back from Tom and began to yell loudly. "Help! Help! Someone is taking the Chinoises."

Three men had been watching the fight from the far end of the block. At the call, they broke into a run along the street.

Tom thought of grabbing Chun and running in the opposite direction; however, she could never outdistance the men. He put his hand under his coat and on the butt of his six-gun.

He tried to speak to Chun, but his mouth was full of blood. He spewed it out in a spray of red droplets. He hoped his teeth were not broken.

"Come here to me," he told Chun.

Hastily she drew near. He took her by the hand and walked steadily forward toward the corner.

Two of the men drew blackjacks from inner pockets. The third pulled a long-bladed knife from a sheath on his belt. The second China-man, also holding a knife, angled in from the side to join his reinforcements. They blocked Tom's way.

"Fellow, that was a right good fight you put up," said a large, sandy-haired man. "But there will be no more fists used." He smacked his blackjack in his hand. "These girls are our busi-ness and if we let one go, they all will want out. We can't allow that. So just give us this pretty one and go buy yourself one. There are plenty to be had and cheap."

"Go to hell," growled Tom.

"Spread out and let's take him," snarled a second man.

Tom pulled his pistol from under his coat. He pointed it at first one man and then another, letting each of them look down the black, open hole of the barrel.

"Nobody is going to hit me or cut me, and I'm leaving here with this girl. Any man that tries to stop me will get a bullet through his ugly face.

"You! Move out of the way," Tom snapped at the sandy-haired man. "I'm going right down the center of the street. I hope one of you starts something. I'm damn mad and want an excuse to shoot one of you."

The man stepped grudgingly from Tom's path. "If I had a gun, I'd send you to hell."

"Go and get one," Tom said. "I'll wait." He laughed, his bloody face an evil mask splitting open to smile horribly.

He pivoted to see all the men. The snout of his six-gun pointed here and there like a snake's head looking for something to strike. No man stirred.

Tom led Chun away, glancing back often to check on the actions of the men to insure they could do them no harm.

Finnegan looked up as the door of the station house was flung roughly open. A bloody-faced man stomped in, leading a painted Chinese whore.

"What in the hell's going on here?" Finnegan croaked angrily. "You damn near broke the door off the hinge."

"I've brought you a present," Tom said. "One of the crib girls wanted to leave there and I helped her."

"So, it's you, Gallatin. You look like a wagon ran over your face." Finnegan looked at Chun and then back at Tom. "What are you feeling so proud about? There's hundreds and hundreds of these whores and you help just one."

Tom was taken aback by Finnegan's harsh response. He was hurt and bloody. His temper flared. "So there's many hundreds of them, Finnegan. Well, how many have you helped?"

The chief of police slowly stood up. His face altered and Tom detected a momentary flash of the strain the job was putting on Finnegan.

"Absolutely none, Tom," he said in a mollifying tone. "What can I do for you?"

"Not me. Help this girl, Chun Zheng. She has no money or place to stay."

"I can do that. There's a woman named Cora

Pendleton who has a large boardinghouse on Tenama Street. She has a crusade going to help whores. She will take in any woman that wants to break away from that business. Take this girl there. Mrs. Pendleton will find work for her and give her a place to live."

"Won't the crib owners and protectors come and take her back?"

"No. I have put out the word that I will personally break the head of any man that bothers Mrs. Pendleton or the girls she has living in her home. The whoremasters know I mean what I say and have never gone near the place."

"All right. I'll take her there."

"I'll go with you. You may need some protection yourself. Did you have to kill anyone to get her free?"

"No. But it was a near thing."

"Good. I'd hate to arrest you for murder and see you stand trial. Did you know two dead Chinamen were found not far from where you live?"

"They probably tried to kill someone and got killed themselves," Tom said.

"Well now, that might be the answer," said Finnegan, thoughtfully looking at Gallatin.

Chapter 10

Tom saddled the black horse and mounted. He sent the long-legged animal at a rocking lope up the hill toward the summit of Mount Sutro.

He had left Chun with Mrs. Pendleton, a smiling, pleasant woman, and then had gone to his apartment. Ging had doctored his injuries and he had changed from his bloody clothing.

She had offered him food, but he refused. Telling her he would return soon, he left, feeling unsettled and troubled.

The horse warmed to its work and its pace grew swifter. Soon it was running a smooth, even gait along the same trail it had traveled the day before. Tom heard the suck and blow of the powerful beast's lungs and felt the bunching and stretching of its muscles between his legs as it lunged onward. As it always did, the sensation of riding soothed him.

The horse stopped of its own volition at the top of Mount Sutro. It rested and blew for a minute to catch its wind and then went on at a walk that gradually built again to a run. Tom did not touch the reins, merely adjusting the sway of his body to the rhythmical stride of the mustang as it ran straight for the ocean.

Coldiron could not sleep. He should have been tired, but was not.

He arose from the bed, quietly left the house, and went to the stables in the rear. He saddled one of the horses and rode out into the street.

The skylight of the stars was still visible over the ocean while morning was breaking on the eastern horizon. A cool breeze blew along the avenue, still damp from the night rain.

Luke rode slowly, heading no place in particular. The city was gradually coming awake and beginning to stir. Men came out of their homes and hurried off on private journeys. Now and then a woman in her long skirts swished by.

He stopped by a tobacconist shop and breathed the pungent aroma as he waited for the proprietor to roll him half a dozen fresh cigars. As the horse carried him about town, he was amazed at the tremendous variety of businesses. They ran the gamut from a harness factory, through a foundry for molding iron castings, laundries, photo studios, wheelwrights, newspapers, banks, to an apothecary shop, the largest he had ever seen and crammed with mysterious bottles and jars.

In the middle of the morning, he was on the west side of the city. He turned the horse and sent it climbing toward a high rise of land three miles or so to the west. Perhaps the ocean could be seen from that vantage point.

*   *   *

Black Drummond felt good as he leaned on the end of the long mahogany bar of The Shark Saloon on The Embarcadero. He was a large man, broad-shouldered with jet-black hair and a beard trimmed short. He ranged his eyes to survey his domain.

The saloon was quite wide and opened upward in a cathedral ceiling for the height of two floors. In the center of the giant room was a polished, wooden dance floor. Twenty couples could swing and promenade to music without being crowded. Surrounding the dance floor was enough space to seat two hundred patrons.

Beyond a chest-high, wooden partition were thirty gaming tables offering monte, faro, blackjack and poker. The tables were rented by the month to professional gamblers.

The second floor had a balcony fronting inward from rooms on all four sides of the building. His offices and a bedroom where he sometimes slept occupied one wall. The remaining rooms were used by the bar girls to entertain their male customers.

The money he had accumulated from the saloon, shanghaiing sailors, owning crib girls and two fast-sailing ships had made him a rich man. Even though he had to share a portion with a silent partner.

The day was early and the only customers were two young men drinking whiskey at a table near the rear of the barroom. They had been celebrating for half an hour, laughing and joking and telling of their gold strike in the high Sierra Nevada Mountains. One of the daytime bar girls tended them and caught their tips, small pinches of gold dust from their pokes, on her serving tray.

Drummond smiled inside his head as he observed the strong young men. He was a master crimp. He had shanghaied more than twelve hundred seamen and sent them on unwanted voyages to seaports at the end of the world. He would soon take these two fools.

The schooner *Asia Voyager* had arrived in San Francisco harbor three days before. Four seamen had jumped ship the first night and vanished among the tens of thousands of people in the city. The captain had tried to recruit replacements, but with no success. He had sent out the word of his need for four able-bodied seamen. No questions would be asked if they were delivered unconscious. Drummond planned to fill the captain's order.

Drummond spoke to the bartender. "Mix two of the house specialties for those men. I'll go get Marie to come and serve the drinks to them."

"They must have at least five hundred dollars of gold still in their pokes," said the bartender.

"Then that's what we'll charge them for the drinks," said Drummond.

The bartender chuckled and began to mix a concoction of whiskey, brandy and gin heavily laced with opium.

Drummond returned from a back room with a pretty blond woman. He spoke to her. "Marie, take these drinks to those two men. Tell them they are on the house. Talk them into drinking them. They'll be flat on their backs in five minutes."

"They look easy," said the blond woman.

"Go start mopping at the door," Drummond said to the bartender. "Tell any customer that tries to come in that he must wait until you are finished and the floor dries."

"Sure," replied the bartender. He looked toward the door. "Here comes Turner. He 'ppears mighty worried."

A sandy-haired man came across the saloon. He glanced at the two young men and Marie approaching them with drinks. He stopped beside Drummond.

"What's wrong, Turner?" Drummond questioned.

"It's that Gallatin fellow. He's just took one of our crib girls. That new one we bought off the Chinaman Yang."

"Why didn't you and the other men stop him? That's what we are paying you for."

"Some of them tried. Gallatin knocked the hell out of two and pulled a six-gun on the rest of us. He's a mean son of a bitch. He really wanted to kill somebody."

"He's already killed our ship captain, Douchane." Drummond thoughtfully rubbed his chin. Had Yang known Gallatin would come for the girl? Or was it as the Chinaman had said, that he could not control Gallatin. Drummond wished his partner, Dan Tarter, was present instead of sleeping off an all-night poker game. They should plan together how to best handle Gallatin.

"Where is Gallatin now?"

"I followed him when he left the crib area.

First he went to the police station. Then him and Finnegan and the girl came out and went to that Pendleton woman's home. The girl was left there. Gallatin then walked to his place and a while later rode off on horseback toward Mount Sutro."

"We can't go for the girl. Finnegan wouldn't stand for that. But I've had enough of Gallatin. Take two men with you and go kill the bastard. Now he's damn good with a handgun, as Douchane found out. So use rifles. Stay a distance off from him and shoot the hell out of him. Bury him out there on Sutro, someplace where no one will ever find him."

"Right," said Turner. He hastened out through the rear of the saloon.

Marie hurried to Drummond. "Those blokes with the gold dust don't want the drinks. They say they've had enough and are leaving."

"Is that so?" Drummond rubbed the scarred knuckles of his hands and walked to the table where the two men were pocketing their change.

Without a word, Drummond folded his bony fingers into a fist and slugged the closest man in the side of the head. The fellow fell with a crash across the table.

"Why in hell did you do that?" asked the second young man, staggering drunkenly as he arose and stared at Drummond with bleary eyes. "My brother didn't do anything to you."

"Neither did you," Drummond said. He reached out, grabbed the man's shirt, and spun him sideways.

Never break a man's jaw that you plan to

shanghai. A man who cannot eat has no value. Drummond hit him in the temple, caught him as he collapsed, and lowered him to the floor.

Drummond blew on his knuckles. He liked to hit people, to feel a solid blow land and the man's eyes go blank. In San Francisco men who were not afraid to use force and violence could take what they wanted. Just be a little cautious, so the tough Finnegan and his little police force did not come after you.

Drummond bent to lift the man from the floor and drape him over his shoulder. Marie pulled the gold pouch from the pocket of the man lying across the table. She flipped the dredges of whiskey from a shot glass and poured it full of the glistening yellow dust.

"Is that okay for my share?" she asked Drummond.

"Sure. It wasn't your fault they wouldn't drink. I've got more work for you later this evening. We need to collect two more men. After that we'll haul them all to the docks."

"A woman could become wealthy working for you."

Drummond evaluated the blond woman. She was one of the prettiest females he had ever seen. And also the most devious and deadly.

"That's right, Marie. Stick with me."

Drummond caught the second man by the collar of his shirt. With ease, carrying one man and dragging one, he took both through a door and down a flight of stairs to a dank basement. He placed the men between pairs of posts anchored solidly in the dirt floor. Stretching the men full length, he bound their hands and feet firmly to the posts. To keep them from shouting for help, Drummond crammed their mouths full of wadded cloth. He stepped back and evaluated his handiwork. No man had ever escaped from his hands.

Drummond returned to the upper floor and leaned on the end of the bar. One of the professional gamblers who rented a card table in The Shark Saloon and the bouncer entered and came to stand at the bar.

"Any action yet this morning?" asked the gambler.

"Nope. Nothing out of the ordinary has happened," Drummond said.

Gallatin sat on a boulder on the edge of the ocean shore and gazed at the turbulent Pacific. A strong wind blew off the water, gusting violently, clawing and tearing at him. The brush field that surrounded him was bowing and quivering to the strike of the wind. His hat was pulled down tightly and his coat was buttoned to hold out the chill.

On the sea, a score of miles distant, a massive storm front was advancing from the northwest. The great cloud bank, purplish black like bruises, blocked out half the sky. A forerunner of mist flew out ahead of the clouds to dim the late morning sun to a faint gray globe.

A booming clamor filled the air as the ocean brawled with the shore. Huge combers of black water rolled in to thunder upon the boulders, to shatter and run long rivulets of swirling salt water in the alleys of sand. Then the gnarled fingers of old water straggled back to the sea to become part of the next inrushing wave.

Tom twisted around to check the position of the black horse he had turned loose to graze the beach grass. It stood with its head raised and staring intently up the slope in the direction of San Francisco. Tom looked behind to see what bothered the animal.

Three horsemen were walking their mounts straight at Tom. With the sound of their movement masked by the noise of the wind, they had closed the distance between them and Tom to a hundred yards or less.

The men held rifles in their hands. When they saw Tom had spotted them, they jerked their weapons to their shoulders.

Tom hurled himself from the boulder. Fragments of lead stung him as bullets burst on the rock. Then he was scrambling away on hands and knees in the brush.

The crash of the rifle shots continued. Bullets sliced through the bushes, shearing limbs on all sides of Tom. A projectile exploded a stem, flinging slivers of wood.

Tom halted after a few yards, his heart thudding, and hunkered close to the ground. The brush field was small, less than half an acre, so he could not move far. His chance of escaping alive was very slim.

He pulled his six-gun, a puny weapon against three men with rifles, and they had the high ground.

The crash of musketry ceased. Tom raised his head cautiously and peered through the top of a screening bush. All the riders were reloading their guns. Quickly, before they finished, there was time for him to shoot.

He raised to his knees and leveled his pistol at a large man in the center of the group. The range was impossibly long and the wind was whipping across the land. He compensated for both conditions as best he could. He fired two placed shots.

The man flinched at the punch of bullets. He tried to say something to his cohorts, but could not speak. He tumbled from the saddle.

The two remaining men yanked up their partially loaded rifles. Tom ducked down. Just before his eyes came below the tops of the bushes, he spied a fourth horseman watching the gunfight from the ridge top.

Tom flung himself in a bruising roll and then a crabwise scuttle from the location where he had fired. Bullets slammed the ground and whined away from the spot he had been an instant before. He felt a momentary gladness he had hurt his enemies and was still alive. But only for a little while.

At times he dared to rise slightly and look at the gunmen. They did not make the same mistake again. One always held a rifle ready to fire while the other reloaded.

Tom noted they were working toward a knoll where they could look down into the brush. Soon there would be no place to hide.

He checked to see how dangerous a position the fourth man was in. He was riding forward at an unhurried pace to join the others. In a moment an additional rifle would be firing at Tom.

The wind shook the brush and hid Tom's

movement as he crawled toward the horsemen. His only chance for survival was to move near enough to have some degree of chance of killing them with his six-gun.

He looked once again to determine the location of his assailants. The two men had reached the top of the high ground. The third was at the bottom of the knoll and beginning to climb. Intent as the first two were on Tom, they had not observed the new arrival.

"There the bastard is," yelled one of the men and pointed at Tom. "We've got him for sure now."

The man at the bottom of the knoll called out in a stentorian voice. "Hey, you fellows with the rifles. Why are you two shooting at that man? Are you lawmen?"

The two men jerked and spun to look in the direction of the unexpected cry. "Where in the hell did he come from?" exclaimed one of the men.

"That doesn't make any difference. We'll kill the nosy son of a bitch, too." Both rifles swung around toward the man.

Tom did not see the man draw. The pistol was suddenly in his hand and he was firing up the slope at the riflemen.

Once, twice, the six-gun cracked. Invisible hammer blows struck the men, knocking them from the backs of their mounts. The horses, spooked by the crashing guns, dashed away along the beach. To stop at a couple of hundred yards distant and stare back, their eyes wide and ears thrust forward.

The lone gunman faced about and watched Tom climb up from the brush. He raised a hand to Tom and then dismounted to walk from one crumpled body to the next. He examined each for a moment and then came through the brush to where Tom stood.

"They weren't lawmen," Coldiron said to Gallatin. "I looked in their pockets and found out their names were Turner, Mull and Saxton. Do you know them?"

"No. The fellow I shot resembled a man I saw yesterday."

"What was the gunfight about?"

"I'm not certain," replied Tom. His face betrayed a trouble he was not quite able to hide.

"You mean three men tried to kill you and you don't know the reason?"

"There could have been several causes for it."

"Try telling me about them," said Luke.

"First, I'm Tom Gallatin. I don't know why you helped me, but I'd like to thank you for saving my life."

"I'm Luke Coldiron." The man made no further statement as to why he had entered the battle.

"Those men could've been after me because I took a girl from a whore's crib. I had a fight with several of the protectors and pulled a gun on some."

"Those are the kind of men that would want revenge," said Coldiron.

"A couple of days ago, I had a duel on Angel Island. A ship's captain challenged me. I had to shoot the fellow."

Coldiron examined Tom more closely. "I heard about that from a friend. There was a rumor the captain gave bad food to some Chinamen passengers and poisoned several. Is that why you fought him?"

"Yes. Except I learned later, from a man I believe told me the truth, that there were no deaths on that ship from spoiled food."

Luke grinned crookedly. "So you killed a man for no good reason."

Tom ranged his sight out over the ocean to stare at the storm working nearer the land. Finally he answered. "I think I did. I'm truly sorry about that."

"You seem to draw trouble. How long have you been in San Francisco?"

"Three months, about. I'm finding many things are not what they seem to be."

"Where are you from?"

"Oregon."

"You might want to go back there."

"No. Not for a while. There's a Chinaman named Yang I need to have a serious talk with. He could be mixed up in this in some manner."

Coldiron glanced in the direction of San Francisco. "It's getting nearly noon and I've got a poker game at the Grand Hotel at one o'clock. I'll be riding back to town. Want to travel along with me?"

"I'm going to stay here awhile longer. I've some hard thinking to do."

Coldiron raked his eyes over Tom. "Say nothing about these dead men. I have no time for investigation by the law. These fellows tried to kill you and failed. That is the end of it. I'll run their horses off up the beach so it'll take them longer to get back to their stables."

"My thoughts exactly," agreed Tom.

"Better keep a closer lookout in the future. I might not be around to help you."

"I'll do that. Thanks again."

Luke stepped astride and left, hazing the horses of the dead men ahead of him.

Chapter 11

Tom retrieved his hat from the brush where he had lost it and walked north on the coastline. The black horse followed. Now and then the animal halted to crop a mouthful of grass and then trotted to catch up with the man.

The storm pushed shoreward. The wind increased in velocity and on its back carried the drumming noise of the great rain beating the ocean a mile or so away. The waves grew to tall sea hills charging far up the sloping beach.

At a high, storm-cut cliff on a point of land, Tom had to veer away from the shoreline and climb up and over the backbone of a low ridge. A hundred feet below him, in a protected nook of the beach, a colony of seals huddled together out of the reach of the wind and waves.

Once past the cliff, Tom walked close to the upper limit of the storm terrace. He had almost arrived at the lighthouse at the Presidio when the biting wind became a gale and came up off the sea and onto the land. Tom slid into his slicker barely in time to ward off most of the deluge of rain that trailed immediately behind the wind. The mist and large drops of rain filled the air so full of water it was nearly impossible to breathe.

Tom halted and squinted into the wind to watch the rainscape and giant ocean combers drive in to battle with the land. White foam blew from each wave crest and came hurtling in like small white birds striking against the rocks. He kept expecting one to cry out in death or injury.

Tom gained the northernmost point of land and the narrow passage of the Golden Gate. The storm was concentrated here, funneled between the tips of the two peninsulas that almost enclosed San Francisco Bay on the west.

The great rain and wind clouted him and found cold entrance inside his slicker. Spume was picked up from the beach in fluffy, wet masses and flung through the air to hit him. He shoved his sagging hat up and ranged his eyes out in the storm to see if some unlucky ship had been caught in the dangerous channel. All that was visible was the turbulent, liquid mountains of the ocean and the rain.

For a long time he stood with the tempest lashing at him. He felt the violence and cold wetness washing away the clutter in his mind over Douchane's death and Chun's ordeal and his worry for being Yang's guard.

Tom mounted the horse, put the wind to his back, and rode in the direction of San Francisco. He had some tough questions for a Chinaman.

Tom arrived at his apartment in San Francisco in the early night. The rain had slackened to a heavy drizzle and the wind had eased. When he saw the lamplight in the window, he smiled in spite of his coldness. The sea had cast up a wonderful treasure when he found Ging.

At his knock, Ging turned the key in the heavy lock he had installed on the door. She let him in and stood watching him. He did not answer her unasked questions. Instead he pulled her against his soaked body and held her.

"Are you hungry?" she asked, looking up at him.

"Starved. Do I have dry clothes?"

"Yes." She drew slowly away and pointed. "They are there. I will prepare your food while you change."

Before Tom could move, a knock sounded on the door. Someone had been out there in the rain waiting for his return. It could not be a friend, for he had none. He pulled his six-gun.

A man's voice called from the outside. "Tom, this is Tan Ke. Can we talk?"

"Go to that corner," Tom told Ging.

She hastened to do as he directed. Her eyes were wide with alarm.

Tom opened the portal and stepped from in front of it. "Come in, Ke."

The Chinaman moved into the room. He glanced at Ging. A look of disapproval flashed over Ke's face. Then his countenance became indifferent.

"What do you want?" Tom asked.

"Honorable Yang wishes to see you."

"It is late and I am wet from the storm. I will come tomorrow morning." Tom deliberately spoke of delaying the meeting to determine how important it was to Yang and Ke.

"That will not do. Honorable Yang wants to see you tonight."

"Why must it be now?"

"He did not tell me," replied Ke.

You are a liar, thought Tom. "All right. I will be there in an hour. Tell Yang that." Tom was pleased the parley was now. It had been more than two days since he had killed Douchane. He wanted to ask Yang about the lies the Chinamen from the *Sierra Wind* had told. And about Chun being sold.

"In an hour then." Ke bowed and left.

"Please do not go," said Ging, her voice scared. "I feel they mean to harm you."

"You worry for no reason. I will be cautious and safe."

"I do not believe so. You are only one man. I have asked questions of Chinese women about Mingren Yang. Some of the women have heard their men talk of Yang. They are afraid of him and say he is not to be trusted. He has many *boo how doy*, hatchet men, to kill for him."

"Then feed me well for the fight that is coming." Tom tried to laugh lightly, but the sound came out flat and dead.

Coldiron returned from the coast ahead of the storm. He stabled his horse and, obtaining his rain slicker from the Whittiker home, left at once for the Grand Hotel.

When Luke reached the shelter of the hotel,

rain was pounding the ground and streams of muddy water were pouring down the steep hillside streets. Florintin met him in the center of the lobby and welcomed him with a somber nod.

"Nasty day," Florintin said. "I have a message for you from Mr. Whittiker. He was on his way home. He was afraid he might miss you, so he stopped by here and asked that I give you this."

Luke accepted the note. "I'll take my chips now. Are the others here?"

"Yes. You are a little late. I'll get your envelope from the safe."

Luke tore open Whittiker's message. It read— Regarding R. Fallon. I have talked with Stevenson at the Bank of California. Fallon had been to see him about buying a clipper ship. Wanted to borrow money, so Stevenson did some checking on him. The fellow comes from New Orleans as he told us. He is known there as a professional gambler. Also as a master duelist. He has killed or wounded thirty-five men in known duels. Rumor says he has also been in several private duels. He is for hire. If someone wants an enemy dead or laid up with a wound, they hire Fallon. He hunts that person and on some pretext or other insults him until that person challenges him to a duel. They say he is very quick and accurate with a pistol. He has never been wounded. Watch him. Sam.

Coldiron folded the note and put it in his pocket as Florintin came with the packet of chips. "Have you ever fought a duel?" Luke asked.

"Heavens no," exclaimed the startled hotel manager. "I call the police when I have trouble."

"That is a very wise way to handle trouble," said Luke.

He crossed the lobby and climbed the stairway. When he entered the gaming room, the players were at the table and a hand of cards was in play.

Tarter faced the door. His eyes locked for a moment with Luke's and then he looked away with a scowl.

Luke spoke to the group.

"Sorry about being late, but I wouldn't miss this evening's game. It should be downright interesting."

Luke removed his coat. He pulled his hat low over his eyes and seated himself in the one vacant chair. The men occupied the same positions they had previously.

"Andy, please bring me a beef sandwich and a beer," Luke called to the young man. "I'm afraid I missed dinner."

"Yes, sir, Mr. Coldiron," said Andy. He left the room with a quick step.

Coldiron watched the finish of the hand being played. All the men except McCubbin and Fallon had dropped out. McCubbin lost.

Luke entered the play. The game ran the same course as before with Beaulieu and McCubbin losing to the other men. The standoff between Luke and Fallon and Tarter was tense with each betting cautiously and most often dropping out after the opening deal, except when they dealt.

Whittiker came in the late afternoon. He nodded hello to the players and pulled up a chair to watch the game.

"Still raining?" Luke questioned.

"No. It has stopped, but foggy as hell on the streets," replied Whittiker.

Conversation ceased and the game became quiet. The only sound was the riffle of the cards being shuffled and the click of the chips as they were tossed into the pot.

Andy lit the lights of the chandelier. The flickering flames draped a yellow mantle over the players and the table, but left shadows hanging in the far corners of the room.

Andy asked if anyone wanted food. All answered in the negative.

Shortly thereafter, Tarter gulled McCubbin mercilessly and took the last of his chips. The beaten man sat and looked at the hand of cards Tarter spread on the top of the playing surface. He seemed about to say something, but then stood up and hurriedly left the room.

Beaulieu fell victim to Fallon. He shoved his chair noisily back. "I'm going to see how this damn game ends if it lasts till Sunday," he growled.

Coldiron scanned his adversaries. Just you pair of cheating bastards and me. Now that the honest men are out of the play, I'll see how rough you fellows really are.

He estimated the large pile of chips in front of Fallon and judged they represented at least sixty-five thousand dollars. Tarter had accumulated about thirty-five thousand.

Luke dealt an honest hand to the two men and himself. Fallon watched him intently and for an instant looked mystified and disappointed when Luke finished without one underhanded move.

All three men stayed to the opener and drew cards. Small wagers were made and called. Luke won a pot of six hundred dollars.

Fallon also played it aboveboard in his deal. He won a small quantity of chips.

Tarter raked the cards to him. As he stacked them for shuffling, he palmed an ace.

Coldiron's left hand stabbed out to vise the deck of cards. His right dropped below the table to rest on the butt of his six-gun. He had been waiting for one of the men to make a crooked move so he could call them. With all three players prepared to cheat, the game would be a mere mockery and must be ended.

"You palmed a card," Coldiron's voice cracked like a whip. With a powerful twist of his hand he wrenched the deck of cards from the big man's hand and slammed them on the table.

"Goddamn you, Coldiron, you're a liar."

"Open your right hand and show the people the card you have there. Do it now!"

Tarter looked at Fallon. The gunman stared sullenly back. From the very first hand of the game dealt, he had known in some inner recess of his mind that the contest would end in another killing.

They had underestimated Coldiron's skill at poker and probably his quickness with a pistol. Still Fallon felt no doubt about his own speed with a handgun. Tarter and he had made an agreement. The rest of the action was his. Only the shooting remained.

Coldiron had seen the interplay between Tarter and Fallon. Luke arose in one swift movement. His six-gun was in his hand. It pointed directly into Fallon's eyes.

"Stay out of this," warned Coldiron. "Keep your hands on top of the table."

Coldiron cast his glance at Tarter. "Open your hand before I shoot it off."

"No, by God. I'll not." Tarter clamped his thick fingers into a tight knot.

"Suit yourself." Coldiron swung the pistol and, without seeming to aim, fired. The bullet skinned Tarter's knuckles and the burning powder seared his flesh.

"Aiii!" Tarter cried out and flinched away.

"Well, I'll be damned, I missed," Coldiron laughed, more like an animal growling. "I'll just have to try again." He sighted at the man's hand.

"No. No, don't." Tarter spoke quickly. He unclinched his fingers. The ace of diamonds tumbled onto the green felt covering.

"Cheats lose everything," Coldiron told Tarter. He raked the man's chips to his side of the table.

"You dealt crooked a hundred times," Tarter snarled.

Luke grinned wickedly. "You started this double-dealing by feeding Fallon winning hands. When did you hire him to help swindle all of us?"

Coldiron did not wait for an answer. He focused on Fallon. With one sweep of his arm, Luke brought the man's pile of chips across the playing table to mingle with the others. "No one cheats me," he told the gambler. "I claim all one hundred and fifty thousand dollars."

"There's only one way you will ever have all that money. You must take it over a pistol."

"I've figured that would be the way for some time." Luke slid his six-gun into his holster. "Pull your gun when you are ready."

Fallon's eyes flickered. "No. Not like this. My second will arrange the time and place for a duel." His gun was in a shoulder holster. Never could he beat Coldiron drawing from a hip holster. For he had seen the quickness with which the man moved.

"No duel at sunrise, you damn coward. Draw your gun." Coldiron's voice was like metal hitting metal.

Fallon's face blanched. His fingers curled.

Make him fight, thought Coldiron. Do it now and get the game over with. "Why, you're afraid," Coldiron said disgustedly.

The muscles were ridged along Fallon's jaw.

"I will fight you only in the proper manner. As civilized men settle disagreements." Fallon circled the table with a slow and even step. He stopped in front of Coldiron and his hand swung up to strike.

Coldiron caught the arm. He slapped Fallon a resounding smack across the face. Damn silly game. "There now, your rules of dueling have been satisfied. However, a cheat like you should be shot down like a dog."

"We will see who will die," said Fallon, his voice tightly controlled. The imprint of Luke's hand was coming alive on his cheek. "The winner takes all the money. Who is your second?"

"Sam Whittiker," replied Coldiron.

"Tarter shall be mine," Fallon said.

Coldiron spun upon Tarter and, before the man could raise a protective hand, slapped him right and left on the sides of his face. "Get yourself a second, too, Tarter. Don't use Fallon because he will be dead."

The big man shook with rage. His hand began to creep toward the inside of his chest.

"Don't do it, Tarter," called Fallon. "Wait and let me deal with Coldiron."

With a mighty effort Tarter fought to subdue his hot anger. His hands clinched and unclinched and his eyes seemed to bulge with the effort.

"Tarter, we will kill him later," said Fallon. "Come and let's go have a drink."

Both men turned and left the room. Just as he passed through the door, Tarter looked back. His visage was bleak and contorted with his hate.

Coldiron stared after the two men. It was not a good thing to delay a fight that was sure to come.

Florintin ran into the room. "There must not be shooting in the hotel."

"It is over for now," said Luke. "Mr. Florintin, those chips on the table represent the one hundred and fifty thousand dollars that is in the bank. Put them all in one bag and write the names of Coldiron, Fallon and Tarter on the tag. Add these words to the identification, 'To the survivor.' "

Florintin folded up the edges of the felt table

cover, catching both the chips and cards inside, and carried all away with him.

Beaulieu came to stand near Luke. "Kill them for all of us who were cheated. I do not expect my money back. You will have earned it when you have stood in front of both men. Don't underestimate Tarter. He is fast with his hands. He is silent partner with some very crooked men in this town and can get their help to fight you. Their ships are in competition with mine, so I have made it my business to find out about him."

"I will remember that," replied Luke.

"Unfortunately, I will not be here to learn of the outcomes of the duels. Tomorrow I will sail for China on my new ship the *Sea Witch*. I have just been waiting for the card game to end to leave. I hope to set a new sailing record for passage to Canton and return."

"Good luck to you," Luke said.

"And the same for you." Beaulieu left.

"Luke, I had no way of knowing Tarter would try to flimflam you out of your money," Whittiker said.

"Not your fault. You were doing me a favor by putting the game together. I'm hungry. Let's go have something to eat in the hotel dining room. They have a damn fine chef."

"I cannot. Emily has arranged for us to attend a new stage play at the theater. Why don't you come with us?"

"That is not the kind of entertainment for me tonight. I want to see The Embarcadero and the Barbary Coast."

"Be careful. There's still ships in the harbor

waiting for seamen. The crimps and their toughs will be out on the streets and in the saloons and boardinghouses looking for strong men to shanghai."

"I'll take care."

"All right. See you at home later tonight."

Luke went down to the dining room and ate from a buffet of many selections of seafood. He finished and strolled out onto the street.

Chapter 12

Ging shivered in the foggy night that pressed cold about her. She hugged the wall in the deepest shadows and spied on Yang's large building and the side door where Tom had entered. She held her knife open and ready to cut or stab.

Tom had left the apartment shortly after Ke departed. Ging had paced the floor for a minute and then swiftly jerked on her coat. The premonition that Tom was in great danger drove her in a run along the street.

When she saw him pass under a streetlight ahead, she slowed. He would send her back if he found out she was behind. She must follow and watch from the darkness. If he needed help, then rush to aid him. If nothing threatened, he would never know she had come to fight to protect him.

The clatter of iron-shod hooves of a horse and the rattle of wagon wheels upon the ground echoed along the canyon of the street. A light wagon passed Ging. A storm lantern in a metal bracket on the front dimly lit the path of the vehicle. Ging saw a blond-haired woman and two men on the spring seat.

The wagon stopped a half block from the side entrance of Yang's building. The light in the lantern was extinguished. The three people sat silently in the dark.

Tom knocked on the door of Yang's large building. He spoke to a guard through the small porthole, telling him Yang had asked him to come. The locking bolt of the door was drawn back and the thick, wooden panel with reinforcing iron strips swung wide to admit him.

The two usual guards were just inside. Tom was surprised to see a second pair of guards, strangers to him, farther back in the room. One man had a long-bladed knife drawn. A hatchet with the handle cut off at a length of seven or eight inches was in the hands of the second man. Their expressions were grim, their eyes flat and uncaring, for they were men of the warrior tong.

What was happening at Yang's headquarters that required the presence of men whose only purpose in life was to fight and kill?

"You must leave your pistol with us," one of the guards said.

Tom quickly scanned down the rear hallway leading to Yang's office. Had that man ordered him to be disarmed? Behind him, he heard the outside door shoved shut and the bolt rammed home in its slot.

The two hatchet men began to advance on Tom. He whirled around and put his back to the wall.

"Nobody takes my six-gun," Tom said in an

icy voice. His hand moved to rest on the butt of his gun.

He measured his adversaries and laid his strategy for the fight. He would kill the pair of hatchet men first. Then spin right and try to shoot the remaining guards before they could come within striking distance with the knives they always carried. Tom was not certain he could slay them all, for they were very close and could spring upon him in a fraction of a second.

"Give the guards your weapon," said one of the warriors. "That is Honorable Yang's orders."

"No," said Tom. He stabbed a hand at the two men. "Stop right where you are.

"Open the door and let me out," Tom ordered the guard nearest the exit.

"I cannot do that. Honorable Yang wishes to see you."

"Open the door!" Tom barked at the guard. "You want to die?"

The man blinked. He had heard what the white man could do with his pistol. Fear rose close to the surface of his eyes.

"What is going on there?" Yang's voice came from the direction of the front hall.

"He will not give us his weapon," said one of the hatchet men.

"He does not have to. That is Tom Gallatin. He is one of us." Yang glided swiftly forward, his richly embroidered mandarin blouse and pants whispering silkily.

"Tom, come with me. Let us have tea and talk of pretty young women."

Tom glanced to the rear as he accompanied Yang. The hatchet men were staring stonily after him. Tom believed the orders to take weapons had truly applied to him. What would Yang have done with him after he was without his pistol?

They entered Yang's office. He took a seat at a small table.

"Please sit with me." Yang motioned to a chair opposite him. He clapped his hands lightly together once.

A young woman came into the room from a second door. She placed a metal pot of tea and a porcelain cup in front of each man. A plate of cookies was set in the center of the table.

In a leisurely manner Yang poured himself a cup of tea. He selected one of the cookies and took a bite.

Tom also drank tea and ate a cookie. The tea would have been quite bitter without the sweet.

Yang finished the simple repast and looked at Tom. "Tell me about the auction of the slave girls. Did you have any difficulty getting into the sale room?"

"None at all. Your man in the factory knew the way very well. But I did not get to stay and see the sale. I do not have the information you asked me to get." Tom was certain Yang already knew of his sudden departure from the auction. The man seemed to know everything.

"What happened?" Yang's expression was unreadable.

"Zaishing Mo, the man that brought the slave girls across the ocean, was there at the beginning of the sale. Then when I looked for him again later, he was gone. I was afraid for Ging. So I hurried to keep her safe."

Tom wanted to talk about other matters. "Mingren Yang, why did some of the Chinese men from the *Sierra Wind* lie to me and say there were many deaths on the ship during the voyage, when in truth there was only one?"

"I know of no reason they would lie. They said it happened and I believe it did." Yang knew by the question that Tom's employment in his service was ended. Tom would be informing him of that in a minute. But he was too late. Yang had already sold him.

"I do not believe it. I killed Douchane for no reason. I think you knew there had been no deaths."

Tom rubbed his eyes. There was another question he wanted to ask Yang. But his mind felt fuzzy. Oh, yes. He remembered now. "Why did you sell Chun as a crib whore?"

Tom rubbed his eyes again. There was something contrived about the conversation, and the tea and cookies had tasted strange. And now Yang was watching him in a sly and calculating way.

Yang spoke. "Chun failed to do what I told her."

He saw Tom's eyes, burning like fire in his head, begin to glaze over. The opium in Tom's tea and in the cookie he had taken from his side of the plate was taking its toll on the white man's strength. A minute more and Tom would be defenseless.

Tom listened intently, trying to comprehend Yang's answer to his question. Time seemed to flow slowly around him and the man's words were miles apart. What treachery had the China-man pulled on him?

Tom tried to stand. He staggered, almost fall-ing. Yang had doped him. But damn the man, Tom could still shoot. He drew his gun and looked at Yang. He saw the implacable malevo-lence come into the Chinaman's face.

Tom had to get past the hatchet men and out of the building. Do it now before he collapsed. He lurched and careened sluggishly back along the hall. He kept ramming into the walls, for his eyeballs were set in axle grease, slow-moving, half blind.

Yang followed after him. He shouted at the tong fighters. "Let him out. Do not try to stop him."

Tom heard Yang calling out but could not understand what was said. He waved his six-gun at the hatchet men and they backed away from his path. He should shoot them. One of the guards threw open the outside door.

Tom reeled out onto the sidewalk. He fell to his knees on the wooden planking.

A moment later, a beautiful, fair-haired woman leaned over Tom. "Let me help you," she said. She took his arm and assisted him to his feet. "These two men are friends, lean on them."

The woman's words were garbled, but Tom understood the offer to help. And she was a white woman and could be trusted.

"Thanks," muttered Tom. "The Chinaman doped me with something."

"You're going to shoot someone with that pis-tol. Let me carry it for you," said the woman. She easily wrested it from his hand.

She nodded at the men. One of them slugged Tom in the side of the head with his fist. He sagged between them.

"Dump him in the wagon bed," ordered the woman. "Hurry it. The Chinaman delivered just as he said he would. Drummond will be happy. Now let's get this chump back to The Shark."

The men hoisted Tom up and dumped him roughly in the rear of the wagon. A tarpaulin was tossed over his slack body.

One man lit the lantern as the other reined the horse hard to turn the wagon around in the street. The horse went off at a trot towing the wagon.

Ging almost cried out when she saw Tom stagger into the street and fall. She thought him wounded or dying.

She stayed in the shadows when the white woman jumped down from the wagon with her two male companions to hasten to Tom. They lifted him erect.

Ging's breath became a thin, winter whistle of fear when one of the men hit Tom savagely.

She ran behind the wagon, seeking the shadows, hugging the walls of the buildings lining the avenues. Somehow she must rescue Tom from the peril he was in. Block after block the wagon rattled off ahead of her.

Marie raised her voice and spoke above the sound of the wagon and trotting horse. "That makes three of the four men Drummond wants."

"All of them are young and strong."

"Easy pickings," agreed one of the men.

"Do you want to try for another?" Marie asked.

"Hell, yes," said the man. "This one is knocked out cold and won't give us any trouble. There's still eight to ten blocks to go to reach The Shark. Before we get there, we may get lucky and find an easy one."

"We'd even take a Chinaman," said the second man. "Be a big laugh if we could get one of Yang's hatchet men."

"I don't want to tangle with those fellows," said the first man.

"Slow the horse down to a walk," said Marie. "If we see a man, we'll act like we are newcomers to San Francisco and I'll go ask him how to get to a hotel. You two come up while I have his mind on other matters."

They proceeded unhastily down the mist-shrouded avenue toward The Embarcadero and the waterfront. They passed groups of men moving along the street, but no man alone. Three sailors with three sheets to the wind shouted out in drunken, good-natured cheer to them and passed on.

The shanghaiers approached an intersection and a street lamp dimmed and haloed by the fog.

"Stop by the light," said Marie. "I see a man coming from the direction of Market Street."

"He's dressed fancy," said the first man. "Must be one of the gentry from Nob Hill. Now he could be a rich take with considerable cash in his pocket. And besides, I'd like to send one of those snobs off to sea for a year or two."

Marie laughed. "We'll try to take him. There's nobody in sight. Both of you come fast when he's not watching."

"What trick will you use?"

"I never know until I look in the face of the man. But I will do something to keep him busy so he won't see you two coming."

The wagon halted and Marie hopped down. She walked into the full light of the street lamp.

She called out to the man. "Mister, my name is Abigail Detweiller. My brothers and I are new in San Francisco and we are lost in this confounded fog. Can you tell us how to reach a hotel?"

"Where are you bound?" asked Whittiker. He warily checked the two large men on the wagon. The bulk of his pistol felt comforting in his shoulder holster.

"To Los Angeles. We have a brother there." Marie stepped closer to Whittiker. "Any hotel will do. Where is the nearest one?"

"There are many hotels. Go down Kearney for five blocks or so. You will find some there." Whittiker pointed and for a second looked in the same direction.

Marie moved nearer to him. When Whittiker turned back to her, she hit him in the face. She screamed and struck at him again and again.

Whittiker put up his hands to ward her off. Damn woman had gone crazy, for he had done nothing to provoke her attack. If she were a man, he would knock her head off with his pistol.

Then Whittiker realized his mistake. The pretty woman was a decoy. Where were the men that were with her? He raked the woman aside and reached for his pistol.

The men had leaped down from the high seat

of the wagon at the instant Marie began to strike at Whittiker. They raced the few steps and grabbed him.

A powerful blow slammed Whittiker in the stomach. Another exploded on the side of his head. Stars flew across his mind. Blackness engulfed him.

"You are the very best crimp in all San Francisco," one of the men told Marie as he supported Whittiker's body.

"There is no time for talk. Get the man in the wagon." She lifted her dress tail and scurried up the three high steps and into the wagon.

The men tossed the loose jointed body of Whittiker into the vehicle and covered him with the tarpaulin. They were all laughing as the wagon drove on.

Blocks later the horse was guided down an alleyway. In the center of the block, the wagon halted at the rear entrance of a large building.

"Marie, watch the horse and our passengers while we go inside and tell Drummond of our luck. I'm sure he'll want us to load the other two men and take all of them down to the schooner *Asia Voyager* at the docks."

The men disappeared through the door of The Shark Saloon. A muffled roar of many voices floated out into the alley when the door was opened. Then the sound fell to a muted rumble as the door closed.

The lantern on the wagon cast a wavering glow both ways along the alley. A long shadow of the vehicle stretched to Ging peering around the corner of the building. She crouched low and went up the shadow toward the back of the woman.

Ging had almost reached the tail end of the wagon when her foot grated on gravel and the woman whirled to look. She saw only a small Chinese girl and leaped down to face her.

"Get out of here," ordered Marie in a challenging voice. "None of this concerns you."

"You have hurt Tom Gallatin. He is in there." Ging gestured to the wagon. "Turn him loose."

Marie understood none of the Chinese words, only the name Tom Gallatin. "So one of these blokes is your man. Well, that's too bad. They're both going to sea for a long trip."

Ging took hold of the wagon and started to climb up into the bed. "Tom," she called.

Marie grabbed Ging and slung her backward to the ground. "Now get out of here before I slice you into ribbons." She jerked a knife from a sheath inside her coat and moved upon Ging.

The Chinese girl pulled her knife and pried open the blade. She would free Tom or die in the fight.

Marie glared down at her small opponent. "Why you little heathen whore, I'll show you how to use a knife." She lunged swiftly.

Ging dodged away. Marie came at her again, her long arm stabbing out with the sharp blade.

Ging remembered her father describing the best way to knife-fight. Duck and weave and move sideways, but never straight at or away from your enemy, especially a larger one.

Ging faded to the side and cut at Marie's arm. She felt her blade pierce the woman, but only a minor wound.

Marie yelled out shrilly at the injury. She slashed violently at Ging's face.

A lock of black hair fell from Ging's head as she spun beyond the sweep of the knife. The long reach of the white woman was extremely dangerous. However, Ging now knew she was the quicker.

The two women circled each other in the yellow haze of lantern shine and fog. They cut and stabbed. Their savage battle cries pierced the night like needles.

Ging wounded the American on the shoulder. Almost instantly, that woman's impossibly long arm stretched out with the knife and caught Ging as she jumped aside. Her breath caught as the blade skittered over her ribs.

For a moment they were motionless, glaring through the murky light, their blades poised to strike and hissing their hate in a kind of elemental language that had not been heard since the dawn of man.

The white woman was tiring, her breath came in gulps. She held her knife out at Ging and began to glance at the closed door of The Shark.

Ging knew all would be lost if the men returned. The fight must be ended now.

She gripped her knife and hurled herself at Marie. At the last instant before she was impaled upon the woman's outstretched blade, Ging flung herself to the ground. She rolled toward her foe. As she flopped over, her arm stretched to its limit and drove the sharp steel deeply into the white woman's stomach.

Ging sliced sideways, feeling the keen-edged blade severing muscle. Marie reeled back. A guttural moan escaped her. She teetered as she struggled for balance, then toppled to the alley.

Ging leaped to her feet and scrambled up into the wagon. She jerked the tarpaulin back and knelt over Tom. The unknown man was ignored.

She shook Tom. "Come with me! Get up! Hurry!"

Tom mumbled. His hands came up to touch his head. He tried to rise, but sank back.

Ging slapped him sharply. "Move. Walk. Crawl if that is all you can do."

She mostly dragged him from the wagon. Then helped him to stand. He leaned on her and she almost collapsed beneath his weight.

The wound in Ging's side throbbed with excruciating pain. She felt the wetness of blood that soaked her clothing. But she drove those thoughts from her mind and concentrated on getting Tom away from the hazardous place.

With Ging supporting Tom, they stumbled to the entrance of the alley. Ging looked ahead. A tall white man in a broad-brimmed hat stood in the fog and blocked her path. He came toward her.

Ging let Tom slump to the dirt of the alley. She cringed back from the big American, for he was a giant to her. Then she stepped between him and Tom. She breathed deeply in and out. It was like a shudder. She lifted her knife and prepared to fight this new enemy.

Chapter 13

Luke stopped when he heard the shrill yells coming from the alleyway behind The Shark Saloon on The Embarcadero. He looked toward the wash of lantern light and saw two women striking at each other with knives and screeching cries of hate and defiance. The bodies of the combatants, distorted by the fog and flickering light, were misshapen and animal-like.

The smaller, quicker woman killed her adversary. She sprang up into a wagon and helped a man down. They struggled up the alley.

Luke recognized the attempt to rescue the man. The way the woman looked back at the door told of the imminent arrival of somebody who would stop the escape.

He moved to aid her with her burden. She misunderstood his intention and he saw the fear and hopelessness in her face. Then that pretty face became fierce and she came forward to fight him with her knife.

"Let me help you carry him," Luke said.

She flashed her knife, warning him off, and spoke rapidly in Chinese. She had splendid courage, for he could easily take the knife and kill her.

He pointed at himself then at the body of the man and motioned along the street. She wavered, studying his shadowy face. He pulled his pistol. Her knife rose and he thought she was going to charge straight into the mouth of the gun.

Swiftly he reversed the weapon and held it out to her. She reached out to take it, then drew back. She nodded her understanding and acceptance of his offer and bent to help him raise the man.

Luke slung the unconscious body over his shoulder. The Chinese girl started off at a swift walk up the street. Behind them came shouts and curses and the sound of running feet.

Ging turned in through an open gateway and stopped in the deep darkness of someone's small, private yard. Luke trailed her in and they stood close together and listened to the search spill out on the street. It was short-lived and the men hastened back into the alley.

A minute passed and the wagon came out onto the street, went the half block to The Embarcadero and off along the end of the docks.

Luke wondered how many shanghaied men the wagon carried. What ship waited? What distant, foreign port were they bound for?

He picked up his load. "We can go now," he said. The man moaned as Luke struck out behind the hurrying figure of the girl.

Three blocks later on a different avenue, Luke laid the man down underneath a streetlight. He was astounded to see the countenance of the young man he had met on the ocean shore.

"It is Tom Gallatin," he said to the girl.

"Tom Gallatin," she repeated in agreement and smiled in a very pleased way.

"Wake up, fellow," Luke said to Tom and shook him vigorously. "I can't carry you clear across town."

Tom muttered unintelligibly and endeavored to sit up. Luke raised him to sit against the base of the street lamp post.

"Shake it off, whatever they gave you. That little bruise on the head shouldn't keep you out this long."

"Coldiron, is that you?" mumbled Tom.

"Yes. I helped this little lady save your hide. Can't you stay out of trouble?

Tom's eyes fluttered and he strove to force them open. "The Chinaman's tea and cookies had something in them. My head is a little clearer. Help me to stand up."

He wobbled on his feet. His muscles felt like wet strings. With the strong arm of Luke, he stood erect. "I think I'll live. Help me a little, and I can walk."

Held upright between Luke and Ging, Tom navigated the six blocks to Mason Street. They entered the apartment and Tom sat on the edge of the bed.

He looked at Ging. "My God. You are hurt," he exclaimed. "Why didn't you say something?"

"Would that have changed anything? I wanted you safe. Now my wound can be treated."

"Let me see how bad it is."

She removed her coat and unbuttoned the front of her dress. The knife had cut a groove over her ribs on the left side. The wound gaped open and blood oozed steadily, drenching the fabric of her dress.

"It will need stitches and soon," Luke said. "Where is the nearest doctor?"

"Four blocks north," Tom replied. "Would you take her there? The doctor lives in the same building as his office."

"Be glad to. When I get back, I want to tell you how she fought to free you. She is a very brave woman. You should be proud to have such a friend."

Tom stood in the open doorway and watched after Luke and Ging. He inhaled the cool air, trying to throw off the effects of the opium and the harm done by the blow to his head. He felt their damage receding and his strength returning. He closed the door and lay down on the bed.

After a time that seemed barely a minute, a knock woke Tom. Luke and Ging entered. She smiled at him.

"The doctor was very skilled," Ging said. "I will heal quickly.

"That is good," Tom said in Chinese. "Now I want you and Luke to tell me what happened. I remember almost nothing after leaving Yang's place." He faced Luke and shifted to English. "I have asked Ging to tell me how it is I'm still in San Francisco and alive."

"She is the one that did the fighting. I only packed you. Let her describe the battle she fought."

Tom listened to Ging's brief recounting of the event. He told her, "Thank you for keeping me from being shanghaied to God knows what seaport," he told her.

"I merely tried to repay you for the night you pulled me from the sea," Ging responded. "There was a second man in the wagon. Those mean people tricked him and hit him very hard. I could not help him."

Tom spoke to Luke. "Ging says there was another man in the wagon with me. He was captured on the street."

"The fellow will wake up at sea with a hell of a headache," Luke said. He began to tell his tale of Ging's rescue of Tom, amplifying upon the valiant fight she had made in the foggy alley.

Luke arose. He was no longer needed here. "I have things to do and places to see." He grinned at Tom. "Stay out of trouble if you can." He left.

Tom locked the door behind Coldiron. Tomorrow he would hunt the men who had tricked him and tried to shanghai him away to a foreign land. He would inflict terrible punishment on them.

He turned to look at Ging. A strange brilliance was in her eyes, drawing him to the bed beside her. His hands came up and caressed her face, the dusky skin, smooth beneath his fingers, like silk. Her eyes, beautiful as pure black crystals, gazed tenderly back at him.

"If you were not hurt, I would make love to you," Tom said.

He saw the smile come into her tremulous eyes. She reached out and, softly as a butterfly's wings, touched his cheeks, his eyelids, his temples. "Make love gently," she whispered.

"Tom, wake up. It's Coldiron. Open the door."

*   *   *

Tom jerked to consciousness. He hurried to slip into his clothes and unlock the door. He beckoned Luke inside.

"My friend, Sam Whittiker, is missing," Luke said. "He should have gone home after he watched a card game in the Grand Hotel. That would have been early in the evening. Ging said there was another man in the wagon. That the shanghaiers took him off the street. That would have been about the same time Sam was passing through that area of town. Have her describe the second man."

"What did the other man in the wagon look like?" Tom asked Ging in her language.

"I do not know what his appearance was. I thought only of you."

"What kind of clothing was he wearing?"

"White man's clothes. With a white shirt. Oh, yes, his shoes were of a low style, not like your boots."

"Think. Did he have a beard?"

"No beard. He had a square face. Black hair, maybe brown, but black in the night."

As Ging talked, Tom translated.

Luke spoke. "How old was he? Ask her how old."

"As old as you," she said, and pointed at Luke.

"It could be Sam," Luke said. "But he has lived in San Francisco for years. He knew the dangers. You say she saw them knock the man out?"

Ging described the blond woman's trick on the man.

"Sam could have been fooled by a trick like

that and the two men catch him unaware," Luke said. "I'm going to The Shark Saloon and make them tell me who the man was. They would search him and know his name. If it's Sam, I've got to get him back."

"I'll go with you," Tom said. "I don't have a gun."

"I suspect we may have need for one. There's an extra in my duffle at Whittiker's. We'll go by there and get it. Then we'll go to The Embarcadero."

"I will return in a few hours," Tom told Ging. He donned his coat and followed Coldiron.

Tom checked the sky. It was clear and stars sparkled coldly. The moon was on the western edge of the night. Daylight would arrive in an hour or so.

Luke measured the distance with swift, long strides. Tom matched him. The blocks fell away behind.

At Sam Whittiker's house, Luke gave Tom a .44 caliber Colt revolver. The two men left promptly.

The lights in the chandeliers were still lighted in The Shark Saloon when Coldiron and Gallatin entered. They halted at the door and scanned the interior. The barroom was deserted; a swamper mopped the wooden floor. Two games of poker were being played behind the wooden partition. All the other gambling devices were stilled.

The swamper raised his sight from his work as Luke and Tom entered. "Sorry, gents, the saloon is closed for a few hours till we get it cleaned up some."

"We don't want a drink," Luke said. "Who owns this fine saloon?"

"Black Drummond," said the swamper and straightened to lean on the mop handle.

"Does he like money? If so, we've got a money-making deal for him."

The swamper grinned. "Better than most people. Already he has his fair-size poke full."

Luke pointed at the doors on the second floor. "His office up there?"

"Yes. But he had a long night. He's bedded down now."

Luke noted the man's eyes flick up at one of the doors of the second floor. Drummond must have a bedroom there. Luke started for the stairs.

"No one dare wake him until he gets his sleep out," said the swamper.

"I'll wake him easy-like," responded Luke, still moving forward.

"You can't go up there," said the swamper. He dropped his mop and hurried to intercept Luke and Tom.

"Sure we can," said Luke. His hand swung up with a six-gun to point at the saloon man. Now that the action had begun, it must be carried out speedily.

"Don't talk any louder than a whisper until I tell you to. Go up the stairs ahead of me to Drummond's room. Quiet now. Very quiet."

The swamper led the way to one of the rooms and stopped. He looked at Coldiron and whispered. "Drummond will kill me for this."

"Maybe not after we finish with him," said Coldiron. "Tell him Captain Coldiron is here and wants to talk about buying six seamen."

The man knocked timidly. "Mr. Drummond, there's a Captain Coldiron here and he wants to talk about getting some seamen."

"Damn you, Finley. You know better than to wake me. Get the hell back downstairs and let me sleep."

"Drummond, this is Captain Coldiron. I need six able-bodied seamen by morning tide one day from now. I hear you are the best man to fill out my crew. I've a large bonus coming if I can make a quick return trip to the east coast. I'd share that with any man that would help me."

Drummond was quiet for a minute, then he called back. "Finley, take the captain to my office. I'll be there shortly."

"Thanks, Drummond," Coldiron said to the closed door. "This will be profitable to you." He motioned to Finley to lead the way.

"This is Drummond's office," said Finley.

"Will there be anyone in there?" asked Luke.

"Not now. The bookkeeper will be in about nine o'clock. He has the next office. It is connected to Drummond's by an inside door."

"Go in." Luke shoved Finley into the office.

"Tom, check for the bookkeeper," Coldiron said.

"Empty," reported Tom after peering into the adjoining room.

"Then take this fellow in there and tie him up."

Coldiron turned to the swamper. "Make absolutely no noise. We'll be here and hear it. If we have to come and quiet you, I'm sure you won't like how we do it. Do you understand?"

Finley nodded weakly. Tom marched him off ahead.

Coldiron inspected Drummond's office. In a bottom drawer of a desk he found two holsters and pistols. One was a shoulder holster.

When Tom returned, Luke laid the guns on top of the desk. "This shoulder holster and gun could be Sam's."

"The waist belt and gun are mine," said Tom.

"That's more reason to believe Sam was the other man shanghaied last night. Tom, go into the other office until I call. We want Drummond without a fight. If he sees you first thing, he might try to grab a gun and I would have to shoot him."

"Okay." Tom picked up his holster and buckled it on. He pulled the six-gun to examine the cartridges in all the chambers.

Coldiron sat in the chair behind the desk. He removed his wide-brimmed hat and laid it on the floor out of sight. He did not want Drummond to see his riding clothes. He replaced the shoulder holster and pistol in the drawer.

Footsteps sounded on the balcony and Drummond pushed open the door and came inside. A look of displeasure washed over his face when he saw Coldiron behind the desk.

"Well, Captain Coldiron, making yourself right at home, I see," Drummond said mockingly.

"Why not, if we're going to do business," Coldiron said and smiled.

"Who said we were?"

"When you hear what I have to offer, we'll deal. I heard you delivered some seamen for a ship's crew last night. Took one of the men right off the street. Do you still have a few stashed away safe somewhere?"

Drummond studied Coldiron's rugged brown face. The man had seen much tough weather. "I don't know what you're talking about."

"Look, if you are going to play games with me, we're never going to get down to bargaining," said Coldiron. "A certain person told me about last night."

"Maybe that person told you too much."

"A man can never know too much on The Embarcadero. Knowledge of what goes on can keep a man healthy. Can you get me six strong men before daylight one day from now?"

"What are you willing to pay?" Drummond queried.

Coldiron grinned at the crimp as he considered the question. His mind raced to give a plausible answer. If he quoted a price either too high or too low, Drummond would immediately know he was not a ship's captain.

"A thousand dollars American for each man," said Coldiron.

"You are generous," said Drummond. He began to sidle across the room to get a more complete view of the man behind the desk. "What is the name of your ship?" he asked suspiciously.

The price of a thousand dollars had been too high Coldiron realized. Seamen were a cheaper commodity than he had thought would be the case. He had obtained all the information possible in his ruse as a ship's captain.

"No ship," he said. He stood up and pulled his six-gun. "Hold there. I want you to meet a friend of mine."

Drummond halted, tense and alert.

"Tom, come in here," Coldiron called.

The door opened and Tom came in, holding his pistol ready. He felt the tingle and slither of his hate as he looked at the man who had been Yang's cohort in the scheme to dope and beat him.

Luke chucked a thumb at Tom. "Drummond, this is Tom Gallatin, one of the men you tried to shanghai last night."

"So you're Gallatin. Damn you. You didn't have to kil Marie."

Gallatin did not move, staring starkly back. Drummond saw the anger in Tom and recognized the danger. Somehow he had to escape from these men. He had a pistol inside his coat. Dare he try for it?

Coldiron came around the desk and Drummond switched his attention to him. Coldiron's eyes were like frozen spheres of water. Drummond had never seen a man so confident of what he was going to do.

Coldiron reached out and flipped back Drummond's coat and yanked the pistol from its holster, to toss it to Tom. He raised his strong, tough hands and balled them into bony hammers. Swiftly he stepped forward and struck the shanghaier, driving his fist savagely into the man's stomach.

So quick and without warning was the blow given that Drummond had no time to dodge out of its way. He doubled forward over Coldiron's fist in agony.

Knuckles crashed into the side of his face. Another fist slapped him in the back of the neck. His face smacked on the wooden floor.

Instantly his head was jerked up by the hair.

Something hard as a rock drove into his face, breaking his nose.

Through the surf of pain, Drummond saw Coldiron's eyes, remote and merciless.

Drummond grabbed Coldiron's arm and twisted, and at the same time tried to roll to the side to break away. The iron vising hold on his hair held firm. He was wrenched upward to his knees and clouted again. This man was eager to kill him with his hands. There was absolute certainty of it in the man's face.

Drummond had hit many men. Some had fought back. Always he had beaten them easily, pounding them senseless with pleasure. Now, as pain ripped through him, he smelled his own fear for the very first time, and it had a foul odor.

Coldiron hammered Drummond twice more in rapid succession.

Tom grabbed Luke by the shoulder. "Stop. You will kill him."

"That's what I plan to do," responded Luke in a dead, calm voice. He struck the man again.

"Quit it," yelled Tom, and dragged Luke away from the broken and cowering form of the saloon keeper. "He is no good to us dead," said Tom in a low voice.

Luke winked at Tom and spoke so that only he could hear. "I have dealt with horses and men for many years. There are certain kinds of both that can never be simply threatened and have them do what you want. You must let them see and feel death, and only then can you reason with them. Drummond is one of these types. With that many blows I could have easily killed him, had I intended to do that."

Drummond struggled to a sitting position. Blood gushed in a crimson tide down over his lips and chin. It began to pool in his lap. He stared dully at his two enemies.

"Where is Sam Whittiker?" Coldiron asked harshly. "I know you have him."

Drummond shook his addled head.

"Where is Sam Whittiker? Answer or I'll start to work on you again."

Drummond peered out from rapidly swelling eyes. "You are too late. He is on his way to China."

"You lie," stormed Coldiron and knelt in front of the man and cocked his fist. "He is someplace in San Francisco."

Drummond's bloody mouth split into a horrible, broken smile. "He is on his way to China, sure as hell, and nothing can change that. If he doesn't fall overboard or die of some heathen disease, he will be back in a year or so."

"I say you lie. What ship did he sail on?"

"The schooner *Asia Voyager.* She left during the night, soon as we took the seamen to her. The captain thought the police might be coming for the other shanghaied men, since Gallatin had escaped. By now the schooner is through the Golden Gate and full sail to Canton."

Chapter 14

Coldiron squatted in front of the bloody specter of Black Drummond. He believed what the man had said and that Whittiker was miles away at sea.

"Tom, let's go." Coldiron sprang to his feet and ran from The Shark Saloon.

"What do you plan to do?" asked Tom, keeping pace as they sped along the waterfront.

"Is a schooner the fastest ship on the ocean?"

"No. I'd say a three-masted clipper ship is faster. But where can we get one?"

"A man named Beaulieu has a clipper and is leaving this morning. I want to find him before he sails."

Luke increased his speed to a pounding run on the wooden planking of The Embarcadero.

The waterfront was alight with scores of lanterns fastened to posts on the piers and strung on lines between the masts of ships where cargo was being handled.

André Beaulieu stood on the bridge of the *Sea Witch* and gazed in admiration at the slim, racy lines of his new clipper ship. In the light of the lanterns and the brightening twilight, she was a beautiful sculpture of carved ivory.

The *Sea Witch* was designed for speed and Beaulieu had outfitted her in a manner to break the record in sailing time for the run from San Francisco to Canton. Her three tall masts held oversized sails and the rigging had been reinforced to withstand the tremendous wind forces the sea would hurl against them. There would be complaints from the crew because of cramped quarters. The narrow hull, built to cut the water in the most efficient way, gave space for the cargo and scant room for human comfort.

All aspects of the race were nearly in readiness. The cargo had been loaded the day before. Now the last of the fresh provisions for the voyage had come aboard on the back of stevedores.

Beaulieu heard the gurgle of the tide around the pilings as it began to build in its outward flow. He glanced impatiently about for the ship's master.

He saw Captain Branham approaching across the deck of the ship. The man touched the bill of his cap in salute.

"Mr. Beaulieu, the tide has turned and the harbor boats are alongside, ready to warp us away from the dock. We can leave at your orders."

"Thank you, Captain Branham. Once we have cast off, you do not have to clear your orders with me. I have hire you because you are a fine seaman. Now take the *Witch* to Canton as swiftly as possible. I will try to stay out of your way.

"Yes, sir," said the captain.

"Mr. Tubman," he called out to the first mate.

"Yes, sir."

"Douse the lantern lights. We can see well enough without them. Have the deck crew stand by the lines."

"Yes, sir," replied the mate.

"Douse all lanterns and stow away. Stand by to cast off."

A man shouted from the dock. "Hello, *Sea Witch.* Is André Beaulieu aboard?"

Beaulieu walked to the side railing and saw two men running up the pier. He recognized Coldiron.

"Captain Branham, hold for a moment. It seems something important may have happened."

"Yes, sir."

"What is it, Coldiron?" Beaulieu called as the two men stopped beside the ship.

Luke walked to the edge of the pier and looked up at Beaulieu. "I'm glad I caught you."

"Barely. We were just casting off. What do you want?"

"Sam Whittiker has been shanghaied. He left last night on the schooner *Asia Voyager.*"

"Too bad. I hear Captain Ruffton is a tough ship's master. Your friend had better learn to be a seaman very quickly. Some of Ruffton's crew jump ship at every port where he allows shore leave. That's because of his frequent use of the lash."

"The schooner left sometime during the middle of the night. I want you to catch her and bring Whittiker back to San Francisco."

"Coldiron, I know Whittiker and shanghaiing him is a dirty trick. I have never had to buy a shanghaied crewman; however, literally hundreds and hundreds of men are doped or bashed on the head and sent unconscious to sea from San Francisco. Most of them return safely, and much wiser. Whittiker will be back in a few months."

"He has a business and a wife. I'm asking you to overtake the *Asia Voyager* for me."

"It's not that simple. Even if we knew where she was going, there would be thousands of different courses she could sail, depending upon the direction of the wind and how the captain tacked. Also, my ship is very costly to operate. She has a large crew of men and I must pay interest on borrowed money for the purchase of the cargo. Let Whittiker come back on his own."

"I want to charter your ship. What do you say to twenty-five thousand dollars? The exact amount you lost in the poker game. Payable after the duel."

"Suppose you are killed? You are up against men skilled with guns."

"There are no guarantees in life. If I'm killed, then you won't get paid."

Beaulieu looked along The Embarcadero in the direction Coldiron had come. "Who shanghaied Whittiker?"

"Black Drummond."

"Is he dead?"

"No. Just bloodied a little."

"That was a mistake to let him live. He will be waiting to kill you when you return. And he will have several men to help him. Your life isn't worth much with all the enemies you have. You give me a note payable even if you are dead and I will give you ten days' sailing time. But hear me, if just a few miles separate us from the schooner, we will never see her because she will be below the horizon. So five days out and five days back and you will owe me twenty-five thousand dollars. Is that agreeable?"

"How much faster is the *Sea Witch* than the schooner?"

"Three to four knots in a good wind. We can catch her if we can find her."

"Then I agree with the terms," said Coldiron.

"Write it out and sign. I'll have my captain and first mate witness it. Where was the *Asia Voyager* bound?"

"To Canton, China."

"Are both you and this young man going?"

"Are you coming, Tom?" asked Coldiron.

"I wouldn't miss this for anything. But I need somebody to look after a friend of mine while I am gone."

Beaulieu spoke. "A woman, I suppose. Well, tell who and where this woman is to my man Jenkins there on the pier. He is that small man."

Tom talked with Jenkins a moment. The man turned to look at Beaulieu.

"Do as he asks, Jenkins. We will determine the charges when I return."

"Yes, sir, Mr. Beaulieu."

"Come aboard, Coldiron," said Beaulieu. "Make it lively."

"Cast off, Mr. Tubman," said the captain.

"Up gangway," shouted the mate.

He shouted again, "Cast off for'ard. Cast off aft."

Acknowledging ayes drifted back to the bridge.

The men in the harbor boats on the water began to stroke with their oars. The *Sea Witch* drifted away from the dock.

"Men aloft. Make sail."

The topmost sail of each mast unfurled, caught the wind, and bellied out with a loud, popping noise. Other sails billowed as the men worked downward, releasing one sail after another. The *Sea Witch* vibrated with a sudden life and heeled to port. She responded to the helm and swung to a course south of Alcatraz Island. She was free and seemed anxious to race the winds of the world.

The *Sea Witch* ran before the wind pouring from the hard blue sky of the northwest. She had dashed between the massive headlands of the peninsulas that made the Golden Gate and plunged onward into the broad, open sea. The great protected harbor of San Francisco lay miles behind, indistinguishable in the low gray outline of the coast of the continent.

Tom leaned against a mast on the canting deck of the clipper and stared forward. Overhead the canvas, shrewdly canted and angled to catch and harness the wind, snapped and snarled under the powerful thrust. Waves rolled hungrily by, green and deep.

Tom's nose sniffed the wind and his tongue tasted it, tangy and heavy with salt. He marveled at the strength of the wind to drive the huge ship plowing through the sea so swiftly. A white froth wake stretched behind, becoming twisted and contorted by the running waves.

Tom made his way to the bow of the *Witch*. The sleek snout of the vessel sliced the lines of marching waves, exposing for an instant the phosphorescence under the surface. The sea gurgled and foamed and spray splashed up to fall on Tom.

The mate hollered. Feet thumped on the deck as seamen ran to his call. They scrambled up the swaying rigging, and out onto the narrow yardarms to alter sail. The tilt of the ship was so large that to fall was to plunge into the boiling sea.

An old sea dog stopped near Tom and smiled snaggle-toothed at him. He pointed up at the men silhouetted against the sky. "That kind of work is for young fool heads. They haven't yet fell and broke their bones. Me now, I've had my gentle fall and hellish landing on the oak. Might you want to be a seaman?"

"I'm thinking on that now," answered Tom shortly. His stomach felt queasy at the roll and pitch of the ship. He thought he would be sick.

The old seaman looked at Tom's sallow face and walked off chuckling.

Tom moved to a spot where the cold spray did not strike him and found a seat in the sun. He tried to ignore the unpredictable lurches of the *Witch* as she raced westward on the invisible river of air. The wind had a nip and he needed a heavier coat. He wondered where he could borrow one.

Luke came and sat beside Tom. They remained silent, listening to the creak and groan of the mast and rigging and the whistle of the wind cutting itself on the taut ropes and howling onward in its never-ending journey.

"Tom, I know you did not like what I did to Drummond. There was no other way to find out about Whittiker. Drummond most likely has killed more than one man by doping and hitting him. He deserved no pity."

"I know that, Luke. But there is so much violence and meanness everywhere. Almost always it is the weak that are hurt. Think of the hundreds, probably thousands of young women being badly used in San Francisco. Those are the kinds of people that have my pity."

Luke examined the sorrowful countenance of his friend. "You are one of the strong, Tom. Why look so glum?"

"I believe every man can be one of the weak in certain situations. And at other times one of the strong. Ging was one of the strong when she rescued me from Drummond."

"Right. Ging fought bravely. She knew it was a time to use violence and to kill if there was a need. And there was a need. In our world a man's strength and the strength of his friends are what protects him. The law cannot do that. I do not believe it ever can."

"Finnegan said almost the same thing. That the most he can do is to keep San Francisco from exploding."

"Who is Finnegan?"

"Chief of police. I think he is a good policeman and does what he can."

"I would like to meet him," said Luke.

"Beaulieu said Drummond and hired fighters will be waiting when we return," Tom said, glancing into Luke's weathered face. "We should stand together against them."

"All right," said Luke. "I will stand with you when you take your revenge on the Chinaman."

"That is a fair trade," said Tom. "Perhaps we might even win. How long for us to catch the *Asia Voyager* if we are on the same course?"

"Beaulieu and the captain have done some figuring on that question. Of course, the sooner we can overhaul the schooner the better, for then it will have less time to deviate from a straight course from San Francisco to Canton. The earliest we can expect to find them would be tomorrow morning."

"Suppose the captain of the schooner will not give Whittiker up?"

Coldiron's chuckle was mean. "Then we will make him."

Tom lay strapped in his bunk to keep from being thrown out by the heave of the *Witch*. The ship shivered and groaned as it drove through the mountainous waves on the southern edge of a giant storm centered in the Gulf of Alaska.

Each time the clipper struck one of the combers, she staggered and seemed to stop for a second, then she would nose over and plunge into the trough between the ridges of water. To be instantly driven by the great sails into the next oncoming wave.

Captain Branham had not reduced canvas as the sea grew more turbulent. He changed course to a more northerly direction to meet the waves at a steeper angle. He had then sent all the crewmen below to their quarters, except for the duty watch.

Tom had gone down into the bowels of the ship with the men. He had tried to read their faces as to whether they were concerned about the beating the *Witch* was taking. They did not seem to regard the sea or the slam and jar of their vessel as anything unusual.

It was most unusual to Tom. He felt ill. His head ached and the bile of his stomach wanted to come into his mouth. He lay very still. There was an excitement within him to be on the sleek ship and feel the wind and the waves, but until his body adapted to the sickening motion, there was no joy.

Coldiron lay on the adjoining bunk. He slept. The motion of the ship did not appear to bother him. Damn lucky fellow, thought Tom.

The wind came directly from the north, cold and damp. It wailed through the rigging of the *Sea Witch* and snapped the canvas of the sails like pistol shots.

The ship had changed course to the southwest during the night. The huge waves the northern storm had cast up during the night were now a heavy after sea rolling behind the *Sea Witch.*

Tom and Luke were on the bow of the clipper looking past the jibs at the gray horizon. Dawn was breaking in the east. The race across the darkness of the night was nearly finished. Would they see the *Asia Voyager* when the sunlight came?

Captain Branham shouted out from the wheelhouse. "Mr. Tubman, send a lookout aloft to the crow's nest with a spyglass. Tell him to report every sail."

"Aye, Captain," replied Tubman. He turned to a young crewman. "Brady, up you go. Don't drop the glass. It'd be better that you landed in the sea than the glass. We're looking for a schooner."

"Aye, sir. I know. I'll see her if she's there."

Tom saw the sailor climb the rope ladder up the swaying mainmast. The inverted pendulum swing of the crow's nest was magnified a hundredfold from the movement of the deck, perhaps an arc of fifty, sixty feet. Yet the seaman made it safely, pulling himself inside the barrel-shaped platform. He commenced to scan the far, curving horizon.

The blue-gray of dusk was washed away by the glare of the sun. Tom's eyes leaped the miles to his nearer horizon. The ocean was empty.

"We missed the schooner or have not caught up with it," said Luke.

"Too large an ocean to sail for a whole day and night and find one small ship the first thing when daylight comes," Tom said.

"Brady, do you see any ships?" Tubman yelled up at the crow's nest.

"There's a steamer due south and has a heading that will take her to San Francisco," said Brady. "There are no sails."

"Keep your eye working," called Tubman.

"Aye, sir."

Beaulieu came forward to talk with Coldiron. "Nothing but one coal burner and open ocean," Beaulieu said.

"What do you propose we do?" asked Coldiron.

"Captain Branham thinks we may have held

farther north than did the schooner. He will continue our present southwest course for a few hours and see what we find. Let's have some breakfast with hot coffee while we wait." He led the way to the galley.

In mid-morning, Brady shouted down from the crow's nest. "Deck ahoy. Sail on the port bow."

"How's she rigged? Two mast or three?" called Tubman.

"Too far away to tell, sir. She's heading dead away from us.

Branham sent seamen swarming up the masts. The sails were changed a few degrees and the *Witch* brought to port to point directly at the unknown ship. She bound forward on the chase.

An hour later, Brady hollered down. "Two masts. She's schooner-rigged."

The race continued hour by hour, and the distance between the ships diminished. Tom could now see the sails of the other ship from his position on the deck.

"She's a fast one," Beaulieu said, pointing at the schooner scudding away before the wind. "The way she sails, I believe we will find she is the *Asia Voyager*. Captain Ruffton always could get everything a ship had in her. I'm betting he won't let us board him."

He glanced at Coldiron. "Better think of a damn believable reason why he should drop sail and let you come aboard."

"I have," said Coldiron.

Chapter 15

The *Sea Witch*, with every sail drawing mightily, bolted in pursuit of the unidentified schooner. The fiery orb of the sun climbed the sapphire-blue sky to its zenith and walked slowly down along its ancient path. The froth-topped waves gradually died, becoming rolling swells as the ship scurried ever farther from the storm lying in the Gulf of Alaska.

As the sea quieted, a huge white fish rose to the surface and swam a silent race beside the *Sea Witch*. Tom leaned on the safety cable that ran along the outer edge of the deck and watched the giant of the ocean plunge through the water. Always it stayed just below the bottoms of the wave troughs, its form fading in and out as the water deepened and shallowed over its back. With apparent ease, the fish kept pace with the clipper ship for miles. Then for a reason known only to itself, the fish disappeared back into the wet depths with one sweep of its monstrous tail.

The clipper gained steadily on the distant, miniature schooner. In the late afternoon, as the chase wore on, the schooner grew to a real ship with men visible, working on the deck and in the sails.

"Coldiron, it's the *Asia Voyager*," said Beaulieu, lowering his telescope. "I can now make out her name on the stern.

"That's good news," replied Coldiron. "Maybe we can have Whittiker off the schooner yet today."

"It appears we will overtake her before night," Beaulieu said. "The captain of the ship has not made it easy for us to catch him."

"Can you get close enough for me to talk with the captain?"

"Sure. Another half hour should do that."

Luke looked at Tom standing nearby, listening to the conversation. "Now that we know she is the right ship, Tom, let's talk and lay our plan to hoodwink the schooner crew."

"I will probably regret this trip, but I must be part of the whole scheme," said Beaulieu.

The men talked, devising their strategy.

"Tom and I will need seamen's clothing to pull this off," said Coldiron.

"I will get you shoes, pants, jacket and cap from the slop chest," said Beaulieu.

With both ships cutting a white wake, the *Sea Witch* crept up on the starboard side of the *Asia Voyager*. Captain Branham held fifty yards to windward and the tall sails of the clipper threw a wind shadow over the smaller ship. Immediately the hard, full sails of the schooner softened, losing part of their thrust. The vessel slowed.

Crewmen gathered to line the rails of both ships and watch the other vessel. Some of the men raised their hands in greeting.

"That's Ruffton near the helmsman," said Beaulieu. "He's ready to fall away with the wind if we seem to threaten him. Our coming up on him like this has made him cautious. He and part of his crew will be armed."

"Where do they keep their arms?" asked Coldiron.

"In the captain's quarters," said Beaulieu. He lifted the speaking horn and shouted across the water. "Captain Ruffton, this is André Beaulieu, I have a messenger for you from Black Drummond." He handed the horn to Coldiron.

"My name is Coldiron. Drummond asked me to find you if I could and give you information about one of your crewmen. It is important that you have this news. May I come aboard?"

"Tell me what the message is from there," Ruffton called back.

"I do not think that would be wise," shouted Coldiron. "You should hear this alone."

Ruffton paced a short way forward and then returned, all the time watching the unknown man on the *Sea Witch.* Would Beaulieu lead him into danger? The Frenchman was well thought of as a businessman. He usually transported legitimate cargo. However, he also did some smuggling once in a while as did most shipowners and their captains, to sweeten their profits.

Ruffton was armed with a revolver, and so were his first and second officers. That should ensure safety.

He shouted to the *Sea Witch*. "I will lower sail. Prepare to come aboard."

Both ships halted and lay tossing in the swells of the ocean. The captain's gig of the *Sea Witch* was lowered into the water.

"I'll send Daly as your coxswain. He's got the steadiest nerves," Beaulieu told Coldiron.

"He'll need them. If there is shooting, he'll be an easy target just sitting there in the boat."

Daly and four oarsmen, followed by Coldiron and Gallatin, went down the Jacob's ladder into the gig. They shoved off and rowed toward the *Asia Voyager*.

Coldiron climbed the ladder hanging on the side of the schooner and stepped onto the deck. He scanned quickly over the crewmen ganged about and watching curiously. Whittiker was not in sight. Had Drummond tricked him? Was Whittiker on some other ship?

Gallatin came over the side and stood near Coldiron. "Damn lot of men to fight," he said in a low voice.

Luke approached Ruffton. "My name is Coldiron," he said and shook the captain's hand. "Can we talk in private?"

"I suppose so," said Ruffton in a grudging tone. "What in hell could Drummond know that was worth all this trouble?"

"You will understand its importance when you hear it," said Coldiron.

"All right. Come to my cabin." Ruffton pointed a finger at Tom. "You wait here with my two officers."

"Certainly, Captain," Tom said.

Ruffton led aft to his cabin. "What do you want to tell me, Coldiron?" he asked, seating himself on a chair bolted to the deck.

Luke took a chair facing Ruffton. The captain was a man of medium height with a florid complexion. His nose was a round blob, full of prominent veins. He frequently rubbed and pulled at it.

"Drummond has found out one of the men he shanghaied for you in San Francisco is an important person. He is the one named Whittiker. He has friends who will be looking for him and they will cause trouble for you when they find out how he got on your ship. Drummond says I should take the fellow back to San Francisco."

Ruffton laughed mockingly deep in his chest. "I'm in no danger from the law. I've got Whittiker's mark on sailing papers and they're witnessed by my first and second mates. Also, I've paid him twenty dollars in wages and he has made his mark on the ledger for that amount. He's mine for this voyage and it's completely legitimate."

"His friends won't believe he put a mark, for he can write. And they'll know he would not sign willingly. Even if the law can't touch you, they surely can."

"I'm nearly two days at sea. Those friends you talk of are in San Francisco. What can they do?"

"Two of Whittiker's friends are on your ship." Coldiron's gimlet eyes bore into Ruffton.

The captain's visage became hard. An under-

standing look came into his eyes. He leaned
forward toward Coldiron. "I have thirty men.
What can two men do? What can you and the
kid on the deck do?"

"You wouldn't trust your men enough to arm
them. I saw only your officers with guns. That
kid, as you call him, is one of the best gunmen
I have ever seen. He could shoot the hell out of
your crew in a fraction of a second. Your two
officers would be dead before they could touch
their pistols."

"Don't threaten me, for I don't scare."

"Maybe not. But you can die easy as any other
man. Have Whittiker brought here and right
now."

Ruffton felt the hair curl on the back of his
neck as he looked into the glacial face of Coldiron.
He prepared himself to grab the Colt revolver in
his belt.

"Don't do it," warned Coldiron, easily reading
the man's intentions. "I can beat you. I'll knock
your damn head off if I have to draw. You have
kidnapped my friend. I don't take that lightly."

"To hell with you," snarled Ruffton. He flipped
aside his coat and stabbed a hand for his
revolver.

Coldiron's hand blurred. His six-gun came
out. He swung, striking the captain on the side
of the head. He held back part of the force his
anger wanted to put into the blow. Ruffton had
to be able to talk to his crew.

The captain was knocked from his chair. He
fell heavily to the deck.

Coldiron removed Ruffton's pistol and propped
him in a sitting position against a bulkhead.

He reseated himself and waited. Shortly, the man began to stir as he regained consciousness.

"Can you hear me?" Coldiron asked. "I did not hit you hard."

"Yes, damn your soul, I hear you." Ruffton's eyes cracked open and he gingerly touched the swelling lump on the side of his head.

"Then stand up," ordered Coldiron.

The captain climbed slowly erect. Coldiron caught him by the shoulder.

"We're going to walk to the door. You open it and tell your first officer to go get Whittiker and bring him here."

Tom positioned himself with his back to the sea. He unbuttoned his seaman's coat to make his pistol ready to his hand. The two officers, their revolvers stuck in their belts, eyed him warily.

Time dragged by. Tom heard the lap of the sea on the side of the ship. In the edge of his vision, he saw the tall bulk of the clipper ship dipping to the rise and fall of the sea. He concentrated on the two armed men before him. Soon he could be fighting them to the death.

All of the schooner's crew had stopped working, sensing something important was about to happen. Tom saw two young seamen inching in his direction through the crowd. Their faces were bruised. They had similar features and Tom judged them relatives, brothers probably.

The hatchway of the captain's cabin opened. Ruffton called out. "McCraw, bring Whittiker here. Be quick about it."

"Aye," replied one of the men with a pistol. He hurried off along the deck.

A moment later Whittiker came up from a scuttleway onto the deck. He walked unsteadily, slumped forward looking at the deck. The back of his shirt was blood-splotched.

"The captain wants to see you," said the mate. "Go to his cabin."

"What does the bastard want? To flog me again? Well, tell him I'll not work, regardless how many lashes he gives me."

"That kind of talk will sure get you two dozen more," growled the mate. "Now go on. I'll be right behind you."

The captain stood in the hatchway. He spoke to McCraw. "That'll be all. Go back to your post."

"Yes, sir."

"Come here, Whittiker," said Ruffton. "Come inside."

Whittiker stepped through the hatchway and glanced at the two occupants. His lips split into a grin that grew to a smile that encompassed his entire face. "Luke!" he cried. "How in hell did you ever get here?"

"A *Witch* brought me. Are you ready to go back to San Francisco?"

"I guess I'd better, before this crazy man has me flogged to death. He's already got a good start."

"Ruffton, we're leaving. You're going over to the *Sea Witch* with us. If you make no trouble, you can come back to your ship alive. Give one false word to your crew and you are a dead man.

"Sam, take his pistol. We may have to shoot our way off the ship. Kill this man first."

"It would be a pleasure," said Whittiker. He put the end of the barrel of the gun between the captain's eyes. "Give me one reason to shoot. Just a small one."

Coldiron pulled the hatchway open. He nodded at Tom.

Without warning, Tom drew on the armed officers. "Don't move," he commanded. "Put your hands on top of your heads."

The two men stood poised. They looked at the captain's cabin. All they could see was Coldiron in the hatchway. Their hands slowly rose.

Tom took both men's weapons. "Back up out of the way."

"Damn you for pulling a gun on me," growled the first officer as both men moved grudgingly away.

Tom scanned the crew scattered about the deck. "Your captain shanghaied a man that we aim to take back to San Francisco. We have no argument with anyone else. But I will shoot any man that tries to stop us."

The two fellows who could be brothers separated themselves from the other crew members and came nearer to Tom. One spoke. "We have been beaten and shanghaied. I'm Jeff Iverson and that is my brother Albert. Take us with you."

Tom examined the men. To take Whittiker from the ship when you were certain he had been forced aboard was a proper thing to do. These two might simply be jumping ship.

Coldiron, Ruffton and Whittiker came from the cabin. When Coldiron saw the two men talking to Tom, he called out, "What's the problem?"

"These gents say they were shanghaied same as Whittiker," Tom replied. "They want to go with us."

"They tell the truth," said Whittiker. "Let them come."

"Get in the boat," Tom said. "Hurry."

"Ruffton, you go next," ordered Coldiron. "Whittiker, follow him down."

Coldiron faced the crew of the *Asia Voyager.* "We are taking your captain for a little boat ride. Wait five minutes, then lower a boat and come and get him."

"Keep the son of a bitch," said a voice from the rear of the crowd.

Coldiron saw other heads nodding. Ruffton was not a captain liked by his crew.

All the seamen froze as the captain spun about and raked his sight over them. After a few seconds he gave up the attempt to detect the owner of the voice. He pointed a finger at a rawboned crewman. "Thompson, lower my boat and follow."

"Tom, go down to the boat," Coldiron directed. "Help Whittiker down and stand ready to shoot any man that looks over the side."

"Right."

"Now I'm leaving," said Coldiron. "I warn you, don't anybody come to the side of the ship."

He backed to the ship's railing, swept the throng of men with a harsh look, and went down the ladder. He dropped into the gig.

"Daly, let's go. Get us away quickly."

"Damn right," said the coxswain. "Heave your raggedy asses," he snapped at the seamen. He shoved the tiller to the side. The oarsmen dug strongly into the water and the gig sped from the schooner.

Shortly, the boat pulled in under the side of the towering clipper. The men began to climb one by one up the ladder hanging on the hull of the ship.

Whittiker glowered with deadly intent at Ruffton. "I will be waiting in San Francisco for your return. I will settle my score with you then. I would do it now, if my friends would not get into trouble because of it."

Whittiker grabbed hold of the rope of the ladder and started upward. Tom leaned down to help him climb.

"Daly, go put the captain in his own boat," said Coldiron.

The *Sea Witch* drove toward San Francisco in a stiff wind. Tom sat with Luke and Sam on the fantail of the ship and watched astern at the *Asia Voyager* a mile distant.

The sun was a sullen red orb, swelling as it touched the horizon. The schooner had all sails raised and was dashing directly west. Its sails caught the rays of the sun and flamed as if on fire.

"Luke, you and Tom have done more than any man has a right to expect from a friend. The twenty-five thousand dollars' charge for the ship is my debt and I will be pleased to pay it."

"Drummond will be made to pay the cost of the *Sea Witch*," said Coldiron.

"He will not do that willingly," Whittiker replied.

"There will be a fight," agreed Coldiron. "The alternative is to try to have him arrested for shanghaiing you. We might prove it. However, Tom and I did treat him rough and I don't know how the courts would look at that."

"I know the law in San Francisco and Drummond's power. He has remained in business for many years. As crooked as he is, he must be bribing several officials."

"I agree," Tom said. "And I don't think I could have Mingren Yang jailed. We must punish our enemies ourselves."

"Then that is what we will do," Luke said. "We can't let them choose the time and place. We must take the battle to them. We will hit Yang and Drummond before they know we have returned, and then I will settle with Fallon and Tarter."

Tom glanced out over the restless ocean at the sun's red dying. His father had once told him that danger comes cloaked in many forms. Tom knew some of its forms—a sly, lying Chinaman, a shanghaiing saloon keeper and a mercenary sea captain.

Yang was the worst of the lot. He had been thwarted in his attempt to have Tom shanghaied. Drummond would relay that information to Yang quickly. The Chinaman would seek Tom. Only Ging would be found.

Yang, knowing Tom's liking for the girl, would direct his fury upon her. He might send his hatchet men with their sharp-edged weapons to retaliate. Or perhaps with his devious mind, he would contrive something even more horrible.

Tom's heart beat and thrashed within the cage of his ribs like a captive hawk. Fear for Ging hung over him like the shadow of some great bird of darkness that you cannot see, but feel in all your being that it is real. Hurry, *Sea Witch!* Hurry! Tom pleaded silently to the speeding ship.

Chapter 16

Tom paced the deck of the *Sea Witch* as the moon slipped its ground ties and climbed unbridled in the night's black sky. His worry for Ging would not let him rest. In the rush to sail with Luke to rescue Whittiker, Tom had made a terrible mistake. He had left Ging unprotected in San Francisco, when his first duty should have been to shield and keep her safe.

Luke sat in the wheelhouse of the ship talking to Beaulieu. He saw Tom pass along the deck and went outside to walk with him.

"Something bothering you?" Luke asked.

"I believe Mingren Yang will harm Ging because I escaped his trap. In some devilish way, he will try to get back at me by hurting her."

"She is a strong woman. Unless he uses violence on her, she can stand against him."

"Yes, she has much spirit, one of the very rare ones that would die before surrendering. But because of that, her torture and agony will be greater. She is already injured. I must hurry back to San Francisco to guard her from Yang."

"Beaulieu has calculated our position. If the

wind and our speed hold, we should reach San Francisco in little more than a day, probably early in the morning before daylight. We will go first thing to find Ging."

"We will be too late," said Tom. He agonized in his own certainty of what he would discover when he returned.

Luke could think of no way to respond to his young friend. He walked with him for a length of time. "It is late," Luke said quietly. "Let's go below and get some sleep."

"Not yet," said Tom. He turned away along the deck.

The wind gained strength as the night grew old. The liquid ridges of the ocean rose higher. The *Sea Witch* picked up speed, skimming shoreward.

The ship plunged over one large wave and buried her nose in the next oncoming water column, covering her deck to the hatches with the boiling seas. The cold water surged thigh-deep upon Tom. He staggered into the standing rigging and held on to the cables until the sea drained from the ship.

Tom stared at the cold sea and the moon shadows and the huge waves sweeping by. How had Ging swum for miles in such frigid water? She was a magnificent woman.

He felt the chilling wind and his weariness. He went toward the hatchway that led down to the sleeping quarters. In the small hours of the morning, he slept.

The Presidio Lighthouse flashed its gas-fired, white beacon out over the black sea. Captain

Branham held one mile north of the light and came through the Golden Gate with all sails full and drawing. He turned easterly, holding south of the navigation beacon on the southern tip of Alcatraz Island.

The ship sailed without running lights. The captain and officers called their orders in low voices. They dropped the sails and anchored in the dark, half a mile off The Embarcadero.

Coldiron, Whittiker and the Iverson brothers gathered with Beaulieu and Captain Branham on the starboard side of the ship, which was nearest the shore.

"Fine sailing, Captain," Coldiron told Branham. "We are far enough off shore no one will know we have arrived."

"It is midnight," said Branham. "We will be back through the Golden Gate and out to sea long before daylight comes."

"I greatly appreciate that. Whatever we are going to do can best be accomplished by surprise."

"Daly, lower a boat and take our five passengers ashore," Branham ordered the coxswain. "Come back immediately. Talk with no one. Land only at the sea end of Meig's Lumber Pier. No one will be there this time of night."

"Aye, Captain," said Daly. "I'll be back in half an hour."

Coldiron spoke. "Beaulieu, I realize you have made enemies by making this voyage for me. You will be paid. Also, besides the money, I do not forget a favor."

"I will not worry about that kind of enemies," said Beaulieu.

"If you ever need a gun, call on me," said Coldiron. He turned to Whittiker. "Sam, how are you this morning?"

"Stiff as a man of ninety and sore. But damn glad to be home."

Tom came from the bow of the ship where he had been during the entry into the harbor. He joined the group of men near the davits where the gig was being lowered.

"Won't be long until we know that Ging is safe," Luke said.

"It can't be too soon," Tom said.

"Boat's in the water," called Daly.

The seamen rowed cautiously. The only sound was the occasional low rattle of an oar in the oarlocks or the soft gurgle of water at the prow of the boat.

"We are almost there, mates," whispered Daly. "I've got the lights of Market Street lined up. Easy now on the oars. Stand by to fend off the dock.

"There now. Hold fast," ordered Daly. "Up you fellows go. And good luck."

He caught Coldiron by the arm. "No seaman likes those bastards that shanghai men. Shoot them for us."

"I'll do that," promised Coldiron.

Four night lanterns made small yellow holes in the darkness covering the quarter-mile length of pier. The men waded the murk between the pools of light, going silently among the large piles of lumber and beams. They passed several flat-decked lumber ships tied up to the dock, wallowing at their berths and creaking and groaning as they rubbed against the pilings.

At the end of the wharf, Luke spoke to the Iverson brothers. "What do you fellows plan to do?"

"We are not gunmen. We will get a room and lay low until morning. Then back to the mountains and see how rich our gold claims are. Luke, thanks to you and Tom for bringing us back to San Francisco. You saved us from a hell of a long, mean sea trip."

"Glad to be of help to you," replied Luke. Tom nodded his agreement. The two brothers walked swiftly off in the night.

"Sam, can you make it home by yourself?" asked Luke.

"What do you mean? I'm going to help you and Tom fight Drummond and the Chinaman."

"You are not in good enough shape for that."

"You're not going to cut me out of the action. This is my fight, too."

"In your condition you'd be slow. We don't want you killed. Not after just bringing you back from being shanghaied."

Whittiker turned to Tom. "Help me convince Luke I must go with you two. At least against Drummond."

Tom knew the request was a fair one. But Sam was weak and it had been necessary to help him climb the ladder of the ship. He would be clumsy in a fight. The flogging had stiffened his muscles and robbed him of part of his strength.

"Luke is right, Sam. You are weak," said Tom. "You might cause Luke or me to get shot." Tom did not like to speak so harshly to the man.

Sam backed away a step. He started to make a hot retort, then caught himself up short.

"I can get home by myself," he said in resignation. These two men had gambled their lives to help him. He could never be angry at them.

"Luke, let's be going," Tom said impatiently.

Tom and Luke moved swiftly at a long-legged tread through the poorly lighted streets. They turned right off Market Street onto Sutter. Five minutes later they stood on Mason Street.

"Two more blocks to go, Luke. Let's hurry."

"We should go the rest of the way slow and careful," Luke said. "Either Yang or Drummond could have men stationed at your place. It's best if we come in from the west. You go on one side of the street and me on the other. Be ready to shoot."

"There will be a lot of dead men before daylight," Tom said.

The cold white eye of the moon glared grimly down upon the city as they made the circuitous detour and then stole along Mason Street. The flood of the moonlight cast an army of shadows, like silhouette targets on the avenue and in the alleyways.

The solid weight of the six-gun was greatly satisfying in Tom's hand. He felt the desire to kill primed and lurking within him just below the surface, only waiting to see if Ging had been harmed to be triggered.

Tom glided through the gloom and up to his apartment door. Luke came to crouch beside him.

Tom turned the knob of the door. It swung partway open—when it should have been locked.

"Ging, it's Tom."

Only silence answered him. He rammed the

door back violently with his shoulder, to slam the wall as he charged inside.

He flung himself to the side and dropped flat on the floor. He twisted his head left and right, searching for movement, for a target.

The interior of the room took form. It was empty and cold. No fire had burned within it for many hours, perhaps days.

"Come in, Luke," Tom said and stood up. "No one is here."

Coldiron entered and closed the door. Tom scratched a match to life and lit the coal oil lamp.

Tom's memory was distinct and sharp as he glanced about the room. Ging had sat on the bed and watched him leave with Luke. She had made no complaint of his going, just a sadness shadowing her eyes and her sweet voice telling him good-bye.

He must find her. She had to be more than a memory of a very brief dream.

The squat form of a short man rose up from the rooftop of the building across the street from Tom's apartment. Agilely, hand over hand, he slid down the knotted rope to the ground and sped away at a full run.

He stopped at the side entrance of Yang's headquarters and rapped on the door. Quickly he was admitted.

The man hastened along familiar passageways. He noted a light in Yang's office and he went directly there to knock softly on the jamb of the open doorway.

"Honorable Yang, Tom Gallatin has returned," the man said.

"You are certain?"

"Yes, I recognized him even though there was only moonlight. A second man was with him. A stranger to me.

Yang thoughtfully pondered the news. The sly maneuver to dispose of Gallatin by having him shanghaied had not succeeded. Yang must take direct action himself to slay the troublesome young white man.

"Tell Tan Ke to come to me," Yang said.

"Yes, Honorable Yang. At once."

Ke entered the office a moment later. "I have heard that Gallatin has appeared at his apartment," he said.

"He will think we have Ging Ti and come directly here. It is best that we allow him to come inside and then kill him where other white men cannot see it happen."

"That is extremely dangerous. I saw him shoot the ship captain, Douchane, and he is a master with his pistol."

"Our guards have been practicing with handguns. Some of them and also you and I have developed much accuracy. Go select the guards that are the most skilled and assemble them in the warehouse. We must make a well-laid trap for Gallatin. I will be there to give the orders. I will lead the men to insure the battle is won."

"We may not have much time."

"Then hurry."

Ging's clothing was gone. There was no message. Two teacups with dried brown stains in them were on the table.

"She had a visitor and then left," said Tom

and motioned at the cups. "I would guess it was a Chinaman."

"Only one extra cup, so one man. That probably means she left willingly," observed Luke.

"Not necessarily correct. If Mingren Yang or Tan Ke came with their hatchet men, just Yang or Ke would have tea. The guards would not be invited."

"We can go talk with Beaulieu's man, Jenkins, and ask him what happened."

"I don't think Jenkins will have an answer. I believe Yang has Ging. We must go straight to his headquarters."

"You could be wrong."

"I know Yang. I am not wrong. Besides, he tried to have me shipped out to sea. I owe him for that trick."

"Then the sooner we strike him, the better."

"He will have many men guarding his stronghold, at least a dozen. Though most only use knives and other cutting weapons, some have been training to use pistols. It will be a tough fight."

Luke stared at Tom. "Are you telling me I don't have to help you? Well, if so, forget it. Now no more talk. Let's tear his place apart and find Ging. Lead the way."

Tom set off at a rapid pace. He spoke to Luke as they went. "There is no way to get into his building except through one of the doors. There are three of them. All will be guarded. The windows are all on the second floor and have heavy shutters."

"Sounds like a fortress," observed Luke.

Tom staggered as the street lurched beneath his feet. "What was that? I almost fell."

"Me, too," replied Luke.

The street moved again, a rolling, dizzying motion. The buildings on all sides swayed weirdly in the moonlight. The brick chimney of a house broke off at the roofline and came clattering down onto the street.

"An earthquake!" exclaimed Luke. "Get away from the house and out into the center of the street."

The earth beneath their feet shifted, rippling like the waves of the sea. The buildings shook and moaned. Two signs broke loose from their anchors and plunged to the sidewalk. Windows broke and glass fell jingling. More chimneys crashed down. A woman began to scream.

Doors flew open and people poured into the streets. Their scared and wondering cries grew to a wild clamor. A man began to curse and then suddenly started to pray.

"Luke, this is our chance. Run! Run! We must get to Yang's while they are disorganized." Tom streaked away in a flat-out run.

Luke strained mightily to keep abreast of his comrade. He shouted at Tom. "Go straight for Yang. If we can capture him, then we trade for Ging. Do you hear me?"

"Yes! Yes!"

As they wove a course through the milling throng of men and women and children on the street, the earthquake became quiet and the ground firmed and steadied beneath their driving feet.

Tom and Luke swept around the corner of Yang's large headquarters building. The side entrance stood wide with lamplight flooding out.

Two guards were on the sidewalk looking apprehensively about.

"Catch them," yelled Tom. He ran directly at one of the men, caught him over his shoulder, lifted him, drove onward through the doorway.

An inside wall stopped them with a stunning jar. Tom heard and felt the man's head crack on the hard surface.

Tom whirled, his six-gun coming into his hand. Luke had the second guard down on the floor. His fist struck savagely twice into the man's face.

"This way to Yang's office. We'll look there first." Tom darted away along the rear hallway.

"Watch out," shouted Luke. His pistol roared once, twice.

Tom pivoted and pressed against the wall. He saw two hatchet men slumping to the floor in the front hallway.

Tom continued his race toward the rear. He heard Luke's feet thumping behind him. There was no time for slowness and stealth. The shots would have been heard and Yang must be captured in the next few seconds. Before he could hurt Ging. If she was still alive.

They bolted out of the hallway and into the warehouse. Near the middle of the huge room, Yang and Ke and four hatchet men were coming swiftly toward the front of the building.

"Go left and keep moving," yelled Luke. "Shoot as you dodge and weave. Never stand still."

Yang felt the building become solid under his feet as the earthquake subsided. The scared voices of the women and children on the second floor lessened. The earthquake had been but a tremor.

Two pistol shots exploded in the front hallway. A few seconds later Gallatin and another man with pistols drawn burst out into the warehouse.

Gallatin shouted a high, fierce challenging cry.

Yang stopped stone still. Somehow the earthquake had allowed Gallatin entry into the building before the trap could be set. Events were occurring much too quickly. It was now going to be a frontal battle of men and handguns at a short range. This was not the way it should be. The decision of who was to die and who to live was left too much to the whims of the unpredictable gods.

"Use your weapons," Yang yelled at his men. "Kill the white men." He drew his own pistol and fired at Gallatin moving beside a mound of crates near the far wall.

Ke and the four guards turned to directly face the intruders. They began to fire rapidly.

Chapter 17

The warehouse reverberated to the thundering explosions of the firearms. Bullets zipped across the distances separating the fighters. Some ricocheted with whining noises like deadly bees, to thunk into the wooden walls of the building or the boxes and bales of mining supplies.

The man on Yang's left yelled fearfully, grabbed his stomach, and fell backward. Yang did not look. He concentrated on hitting Gallatin with a bullet at the far end of the warehouse.

The two white men had separated from each other and, jinking from side to side at a run, dashed among the mounds of goods. They would slow suddenly and their pistols would crash and smoke. Then they would dodge away.

Two more of Yang's men toppled to the floor. Gallatin and his comrade seemed unhurt.

Yang missed Gallatin with a shot. Then he realized he was shooting too fast and not leading his target. So too were his men, not yet experienced in combat with handguns. And the white men were always moving while his men stood stationary, their attention totally on the use of their pistols.

A chunk of whistling lead thudded into a wooden pillar of the warehouse near Tom. Splinters flew like darts. One stung him on the face. Then he was dodging away.

Coldiron knocked Tan Ke off his feet. Tom aimed at Yang.

The Chinaman felt the stabbing pain as the speeding bullet tore through muscle and bone. He was whirled about and slammed down.

Tom raced up to Yang and knelt beside him. He yanked the injured man roughly over onto his back.

"Where is Ging?" Tom demanded.

Yang looked up with hate and pain. "I will tell you nothing," he said, bubbles of blood bursting on his lips with each word.

The Chinaman was shot in the lungs. Tom had hoped to capture Yang without wounding him so seriously.

Coldiron called, "Tom, here is another one still alive. Maybe he will talk."

Tom looked and saw Luke supporting Ke against a packing crate. He went to hunker beside the man.

Ke saw Tom's face, a mask lined and frozen with fury. An ice shaft formed in the Chinaman's stomach. He was going to die.

"Where is Ging?" questioned Tom and bent threateningly over Ke.

"I do not know. I went with some of my men to take her, but she was gone and I could not locate her."

"You lie," growled Tom.

"We searched and searched and could not find her anyplace."

"You have hidden her somewhere," fumed Tom. "Tell me where she is and I will let you live."

"You are wrong. Believe me, for I would give her to you this moment if I could."

Tom stared into the black eyes of the Chinaman. He was a shrewd liar. Yet somehow Tom knew Ke spoke the truth.

"Then I will go and look for her myself. I will let you live for now. If you have lied to me, I shall return and burn this building down around your head."

"Let's get out of here," shouted Coldiron. "Before the other guards block the outside door and we have to fight our way out."

"If the Chinaman Yang doesn't have Ging, then where is she?" asked Luke, peering into the sad and worried face of Tom. "Who else does she know in San Francisco?"

"No one," replied Tom.

They had sped away from Yang's building and now were several blocks west on Market Street. Tom was staring down across the yellow glows of the hundreds of streetlights of the city. In some refuge there, Ging was hiding.

Clever Ging had known that without the protection of Tom, she was in grave danger. Yang could strike at Tom through her. Or the merchant who had purchased her in China might discover she was still alive and come to take her as his property. Yang knew of Ging's escape from the ship and could inform the merchant of her whereabouts.

So she had vanished. Even Yang with all his spies could not locate her.

Tom recalled his conversations with Ging. In one of those talks lay a clue as to her hiding place. He must sort out that specific information and find her. The one short fragment of time he had spent with her contained a fortune of memories. But they must not be all that he had of her to last a lifetime.

"She knew Sam Whittiker's name and that we were going to try and rescue him," said Luke. "Perhaps she is with Sam's wife at his home."

"Maybe, but that would be a very obvious place for her to go for help. Yang would find her there. Ging is intelligent and would think of a hideaway and a new name that could not easily be unraveled."

"Mrs. Cora Pendleton." Tom's voice rose on a happy note and he laughed.

"What about Mrs. Pendleton?" asked Luke.

"I once helped a girl to leave one of the whore cribs. I didn't know what to do with her, so I took her to the policeman, Finnegan. He told me of a woman who had set up a shelter for singsong girls that wanted to lead straight lives. Finnegan has personally taken it upon himself to protect that woman's house. I told Ging of taking the girl Chun there and what kind of person this Mrs. Pendleton was.

"Luke, I believe Ging is there."

"Then let's check it out. Where is it?"

* * *

Tom and Luke came to the large, two-story rooming house and climbed the steps to the door. Tom lifted the iron knocker and tapped on the door.

Someone carrying a lighted lamp came from the rear of the house to the front foyer. "Who is it?" a woman's voice asked through the door.

"Tom Gallatin, Mrs. Pendleton. Remember me? I was here with Finnegan, the chief of police, when we brought the girl Chun Zheng."

The door opened a crack and Mrs. Pendleton looked out. "We are just getting back to bed after the earth tremor, Mr. Gallatin. Can your visit wait until tomorrow?"

"I wish it could, ma'am, but I'm looking for a Chinese girl named Ging Ti. I thought she might have come here."

"There is no person here by that name."

"She might have used a different name, for she was in danger. She is very pretty and would have come in the last three days."

"I have had only one girl arrive so recently. But her name is Tojen Chi."

"May I see this girl? It would take only a minute. If it is not Ging, I will leave promptly and bother you no more."

"Very well. Since you are a friend of Mr. Finnegan. She will not be asleep yet. Step inside. Please wait there while I go and talk with her."

A moment later, Tom heard someone cry out joyously. Ging bounded down the stairs. She grabbed his hand and gazed at him with her beautiful almond eyes shining.

Tom held her small, firm hand, sharing her

happiness. His heart thudded. He wanted to hug her. He only smiled.

"When the man Jenkins came to the apartment and told me you had gone to sea, I was afraid. But I knew you would return for me," she whispered.

"Yes, always. But I must leave again for just a little while. This time I will not be going on a sea voyage."

Ging's expression saddened. "You have just arrived."

"There is one more job Luke and I must do," Tom said. "Stay here and be safe. I will return in a few hours."

Ging released Tom's hand. "I shall be here. Do not let anything happen to you."

Luke watched silently. He understood none of the conversation between Tom and the girl. However, their faces told him everything. He would have to keep the reckless Tom from getting himself killed. That would not be easy, for their enemies were many and crafty.

Brilliant white gaslights illuminated The Shark Saloon. The musicians on the raised wooden platform played a wild tune and several dancing couples swung and stomped in rhythm to it. Men were lined up shoulder to shoulder at the bar. All the gaming tables were full and men waited for a space to join in.

"It's a gold mine for making money," Tom said to Luke as they surveyed the crush of patrons. "Why would Drummond get involved in shanghaiing men?"

"Maybe he does it because there is no one to

stop him," answered Luke. "It has been easy money."

"But not anymore. For shanghaiing Sam and trying to do it to me is about to cost him."

"I see Tarter and Fallon and Drummond at a card table by the back wall," said Luke.

Tom saw the three men seated by themselves. A small Chinaman was speaking rapidly to Drummond. The saloon keeper's face showed the bruises and scabs from Coldiron's beating.

"I wonder what the Chinaman is telling them," said Tom.

"What happened at Yang's place, I would bet," Luke said and began to walk across the room. "If the fight starts here, I'll take Fallon. He's the light-haired man. You take Drummond. Tarter belongs to which ever of us gets to him first."

Luke saw the wildness rising in Tom as he watched the saloon man. "Never let yourself get so mad that it clouds your judgment," warned Luke. "Let out just enough to keep your courage strong and your hand steady."

"Wise advice," said Tom. He suddenly grinned into the weathered face of Coldiron. He sensed a kinship with the man, like an older brother. "I will not let you down," Tom said.

"I know that. Let me call the action. Do you see the man with the shotgun on the upstairs balcony? And the big bouncer at the end of the bar who is only fingering his drink and is watching everybody else?"

"Yes."

"They are part of Drummond's protection. We must get Tarter and Drummond and their hired duelist out of the saloon if we are going to have any kind of a fair fight."

Luke and Tom wound a path through the press of saloon customers and approached the table where the three men sat. The alert Fallon spotted them first. He laid his cards down and unbuttoned his jacket.

"Coldiron and Gallatin are coming," Fallon said in a flat tone.

Tarter glanced up. He spoke in a low, hard tone to Drummond. "Do nothing. Say nothing." Then he called out in a loud voice. "Well, Coldiron, you have finally showed up."

Luke swept his sight over the seated men. "I took a little sea voyage. With Drummond's help I got Sam Whittiker back. He sends his regards to you, Drummond."

The saloon keeper glared at Coldiron. "We're not done yet, Coldiron."

"You have never said a truer thing. Tom and I have come to finish our business with you and these card cheats. After that is over, I'll go claim my one hundred and fifty thousand dollars."

Tom stood facing in a direction where he could see the bouncer at the bar and the man with the shotgun on the balcony. Both of them were watching Drummond for a signal. Tom did not think there would be one.

"This is not the place to settle this," said Fallon. "Innocent people would get shot."

"And this argument has grown too large, with too many people involved for a duel," Coldiron said.

Tarter rubbed his big hands together. "How

about Angel Island at one hour past daylight? We will settle this once and for all. Gallatin knows the place on the east end. Is that all right for the fight?"

"Anyplace will do," Coldiron said. "But why not outside in the street right now? That way we can get this over with fast."

"Not that way," responded Tarter. "The law would become involved. This is none of their concern. I want no long trials or lockup in their stinking jail. We'll fight, just you two against us."

"Pistols or rifles?" asked Coldiron.

"Pistols?" said Tarter and ranged a questioning view over his cohorts.

They both nodded in the affirmative.

"Pistols only," said Tarter. "It will be a stand up and shoot it out."

"That's agreeable with us," responded Coldiron.

"Tom, walk over to the door and then look back to be sure Drummond's men don't get an idea to take a shot at one of us. I'll see that you get there safe."

"Right," Tom said and pushed swiftly across the room. At the door he pivoted so he could see Drummond's guards.

Luke came leisurely up beside him and they left The Shark Saloon.

"They will cheat, you know," Luke said. "There will be at least one extra man on the island. He will have a rifle."

"How will we take him out of the fight?"

"By being there first, at least two hours ahead of daylight. We will see him land."

* * *

Fallon rose to his feet. He spoke to Tarter. "I think I'll get a few hours of sleep. What time do you want to meet at the wharf to leave for Angel Island?"

"It takes an hour to row to the island. However, I want to be there before Coldiron. Be at the dock half an hour before daylight. We will use one of the boats of the *Sierra Wind* and part of her crew to take us out there."

"I'll be there." Fallon stalked off through the crowded saloon.

"I'm glad he's on our side," said Tarter, watching the gunman leave. "But we need a bigger edge on Coldiron and Gallatin than Fallon. Our man Crofton is an expert with a rifle. Send him out to Angel Island. Tell him to hide in the rocks and help us kill Coldiron and that kid when the fight starts."

"Fallon won't like that."

"What's he going to do after they both are dead?"

"Absolutely nothing," laughed Drummond. "And I like those kinds of odds, four men against two and one of our men hidden in the brush with a rifle."

Tendrils of sea mist rose up like smoke from the water of the bay as Luke and Tom climbed down from the dock and into the charter boat. Without speaking they took seats side by side in the bow.

The coxswain of the boat took hold of the tiller. His two boatmen shoved away from the pier. They found seats one behind the other and settled their oars in the oarlocks. They began to row.

The men of the charter boat had asked no questions except the destination. They had made this same trip several times before, hauling angry men with weapons.

A huge silver moon hung on its downward, westering arc and from its high aerial view eyed San Francisco Bay. In its light Tom saw the wedge of the boat trailing wreaths of fog on either side. He felt the damp cold.

A primal foreboding of his possible death in the coming gun battle arose in Tom. He wondered if Luke was likewise considering the outcome of the fight. Tom looked at his companion.

The deep sockets of Luke's eyes were full of impenetrable darkness. The lines of his face were set and hard.

A mile slid by beneath the stroking oars. The fog grew upward from the water, deepening until only the heads of the men extended above its silver-gray surface. The spectral, bodiless heads glided eerily through the moonlit night.

The boat drove onward toward the dim outline of Angel Island rearing up dark and brooding. Tom recalled his other trip here when he had fought Douchane because of the Chinamen's lies. Then he had pulled Ging from the ocean and had slain a man rather than give her up. He had taken Chun from the whore's crib on the Street Of The Slave Girls. Someone had tried to kill him on the beach for that. He had shot Yang. And now a fight to the death with Drummond and two other men would soon occur. Tom was caught up in terrible, violent actions. He was very pleased that the man Luke Coldiron was by his side.

Tom felt the chill of the fog increase. Every thread of his clothing, every hair of his head and face was jeweled with crystal globules of moisture. He saw Luke flick droplets from his eyebrows like beads of sweat.

"Where do you want to land?" asked the boat coxswain.

"At the meadow on the east end of the island," Tom answered.

"I know the place," said the coxswain.

He swung the tiller over slightly and the boat veered easterly. The oarsmen stroked on to skirt the shore of the island.

"That's the place," said Tom, recognizing the shadowy hillside and swath of flat land near the shore.

"I see it," said the coxswain.

The boat swerved left and a moment later grated upon the gravelly shore. Tom and Luke stepped out.

"Come back at nine," Luke told the boatmen.

"Aye," agreed the coxswain.

The boat pulled away from the land and faded into the mist. Luke and Tom remained by the water until all sound of the boat had died.

They walked over the meadow and climbed up into the boulders and bushes on the hillside. At a distance of fifty yards, they looked back.

The shallow fog had been left behind. It shone as a three- or four-foot silver blanket, lying on the water and lapping up on the edge of the shore. On top of the mist layer, the night was crisp and clear and the round moon was the height of a man above the western horizon.

"This is the range a man with a rifle might choose to hit a target easily in the meadow," said Luke. He led another twenty yards and found a concealed place among some boulders.

They tugged their damp coats more snugly about themselves and stared out over the bay at San Francisco, a faint glow three miles south. They waited. They would have a fourth man to kill if their adversaries sent someone to set up an ambush.

Chapter 18

The night was utterly still. The moon sank until it was only a finger's width from the horizon. Its rays striking upon the droplets of dew on the leaves of the brush glowed a soft silver reflectance.

The first puff of a rising wind came from the west and went off toward the Sierra Nevada Mountains. Luke and Tom turned in unison to look in the direction of the Golden Gate and the Marin Peninsula. Near the distant land, the driving wind was rolling up the fog in front of it in thick billows, leaving the bay brushed clean behind. The thickening mist was rising to obscure and pale the moon to a wan disk.

Below the men, something moved on the fog-shrouded water. A boat with muffed oars ghosted past near the shore and continued on to disappear around the first point of land. A few minutes later, a man came back along the water's edge and crossed the meadow. He started to ascend the hillside.

The man glanced back at the meadow as Luke and Tom had done. At a cluster of boulders, he veered in among them. Tom saw a long, slender object that appeared to be a rifle in the man's hands.

"Don't move from here until I signal," whispered Luke. He dropped to the ground and began to snake away.

As Tom waited, the sun began to crawl up from its nighttime hiding place far below the rim of the world. Echoes of its light lit the high heavens while the earth remained in darkness.

An agonized cry, a guttural sound of death, swiftly cut off, reached Tom. The shadowy figure of Luke climbed erect and motioned for him to come.

They went down the hill to the upper border of the meadow. Both men drew their six-guns and checked the action and the cartridges in the cylinder.

Daylight began to brighten. One spectrum of its light caught a high, thin cloud over the Sierra Nevadas and turned it bloodred.

The front of the fog bank had reached the island and was beginning to devour the western edge of the meadow.

A ship's boat came into view in the morning twilight. It came to a stop against the shore. Tarter, Drummond and Fallon climbed out. The boat was shoved off to be rowed north around the island.

The two groups of duelists surveyed each other across the width of the meadow. Then the wind-driven, phantom billows of sea mist reached the clusters of men, and their forms began to fade and grow indistinct.

"Run!" sharply ordered Luke. "Run with the

fog." Both men dashed away east with the speeding mist.

Pistols crashed at the shore. Bullets zipped past where Luke and Tom had stood a second before.

"Slow down, but don't shoot back," hissed Luke. "We know where they are, but they don't know about us."

"You have a plan? We can't kill our enemies unless we shoot."

Luke moved close to Tom's side. He grinned wickedly at his young friend. "They started the fight without warning. They thought the man with the rifle would finish it for them and they would be safe. But you and I know that the man is dead and now Drummond and the others are in a trap." Luke gestured at the fog.

Tom studied the rushing, swirling fog that wrapped around them. Suddenly he knew Luke's strategy. "Damn fine plan," Tom told his companion.

The wind began to mutter, puffing stronger and stronger. It harried the mist into faster flight.

Luke and Tom stole to the edge of the water and halted to stare upwind across the invisible meadow. They held their six-guns cocked in their hands.

"There are three of them and two of us," whispered Luke. "Fallon is mine. Drummond yours. Tarter last. Kill them. Shoot until all are down."

They heard voices in the hollow pall of the fog. The words could not be understood.

A minute passed. Then a second and a third. The wet fog hurried past.

"Soon now," murmured Luke.

The fog, pressed by the fresh wind, became more dense for an instant. Then like a curtain drawn, the mist was speeding off with the breeze. The sun burst full strength upon the meadow.

The three men were brightly illuminated in the rays of the sun a fraction of a second before Luke and Tom became exposed. The groups were much closer together than Tom had thought they would be, with not more than a hundred feet separating them.

Fallon faced to the east, Drummond north up the slope and Tarter stood guard to the west.

Fallon saw Luke and Tom materialize as the fog swept away. He yelled and lifted his pistol.

Tom heard the explosion of Luke's gun and immediately the soft crushing sound of lead striking into flesh. Fallon emitted a short gasp and tumbled backward.

Drummond pivoted right. Before he could bring his gun around, Tom's bullet drove into the side of his rib cage and exploded the throbbing heart. He fell loosely to the ground.

Tarter dropped to his knees as he whirled to face his assailants. His pistol swung speedily.

"Mine," snapped Luke. Tarter's movements were very fast for a big man.

Tarter's weapon had almost made its arc, but he knew he was too late. His eyes were wide in fear.

Luke's gun bucked in his hand. A hole appeared in Tarter's forehead and his hat whisked away. He was thrown backward. He twitched and then went slack and lifeless.

Tom and Luke remained perfectly still, staring at the motionless forms that had once been men.

Tom breathed deeply in and out. "The fog gave us all the advantage," he told Luke. "They never had a chance."

"Just exactly as we planned," replied Luke. "The object is not to fight, but to kill your foes without losing your own life."

The killing had left Tom cold, very cold in the center of his being. He faced the sun to warm himself. After a moment, he walked to the upper edge of the meadow and found a seat on a rock. In the rays of the mild sunshine, he felt himself reviving, like a bug after a storm.

Luke came and sat beside Tom. "There are many such rogues, scoundrels and murderers in San Francisco. They prey upon the weak and the unsuspecting people."

"Too many of them. Far too many," agreed Tom.

They sat quietly together for a time, watching the wind over the bay tearing the mist into long white shreds and sending it streaming.

"The boats will soon be here," said Luke.

Tom did not respond. The sun continued to heat the island. He watched a butterfly, the first of the spring, flutter by, a dancer without a partner.

Tom thought of Ging, the softness and tenderness of her and her valiant fighting spirit. The pleasant memories filled his mind and quieted his turmoil. People like her needed to be protected.

"I'm going to become a policeman," Tom told Luke. "I have been thinking about it ever since Finnegan offered me a job. I will stay in San Francisco and make my home here."

"You will make a good Fearless Charlie. You are very quick and accurate with a six-gun."

"I do not like to fight with guns and kill men."

"Because of that, you will make a good policeman."

"With the help of a certain woman I will," Tom said. He smiled at the thought.

THE FAR
BATTLEGROUND

F.M. PARKER

1847. The Mexican War. The Texas Rangers, under the command of U.S. Army General Winfield Scott, battle General Santa Ana's feared Mexican Lancers for control of Mexico City. Building on his reputation as one of the finest novelists of the Old West, F.M. Parker tells a rousing and rugged tale that brings together two men of honor and conviction—Lieutenant Thomas Cavillin of the Rangers, and Lieutenant Matthew Chilton of the U.S. Cavalry's Dragoons—in a bloody confrontation that tests their loyalty and trust.

JOIN THE F.M. PARKER FAN CLUB!
Keep up on his research, upcoming
books, and true-life adventures.

He writes of a time when men lived or died by their guns, when hard men fought to conquer a rugged frontier, and when the words honor and heroism had real meaning—F.M. Parker, the most exciting western writer in years with such triumphs as *Skinner*, *The Searcher*, and *The Shadow of the Wolf*, is now penning a fact-filled newsletter specially for the fans of his western novels. And it's free!

For more information, write to:

F.M. Parker Newsletter
NAL PROMOTION DEPARTMENT
1633 Broadway
New York, NY 10019